"None of this drama is necessary, Luke."

His rejection scored across her heart like the cruelest of whips. All she could see of his face was the angular line of his jaw, as obdurate as his character. She should have expected this; she, of all people, knew how hard he could be.

"You can't stop me. There's no way you can run me out of town this time."

Then he kissed her.

ROBYN DONALD has always lived in Northland, New Zealand, initially on her father's stud farm at Warkworth, then in the Bay of Islands, an area of great natural beauty where she lives today with her husband and ebullient and mostly Labrador dog. She resigned her teaching position when she found she enjoyed writing romances more, and now spends any time not writing in reading, gardening, traveling, and writing letters to keep up with her two adult children and her friends.

Books by Robyn Donald

HARLEQUIN PRESENTS PLUS
1755—TIGER EYES

HARLEQUIN PRESENTS
1666—PARADISE LOST
1699—ISLAND ENCHANTMENT
1714—THE COLOUR OF MIDNIGHT
1735—DARK FIRE

Don't miss any of our special offers. Write to us at the following address for information on our newest releases.

Harlequin Reader Service
U.S.: 3010 Walden Ave., P.O. Box 1325, Buffalo, NY 14269
Canadian: P.O. Box 609, Fort Erie, Ont. L2A 5X3

Robyn Donald

Element of Risk

Harlequin Books

TORONTO • NEW YORK • LONDON
AMSTERDAM • PARIS • SYDNEY • HAMBURG
STOCKHOLM • ATHENS • TOKYO • MILAN
MADRID • WARSAW • BUDAPEST • AUCKLAND

For Mandy, who owns the real crystal

ISBN 0-373-11803-1

ELEMENT OF RISK

First North American Publication 1996.

Copyright © 1994 by Robyn Donald.

PROLOGUE

PERDITA GLADSTONE smoothed moisturiser on to her famous translucent skin, then glanced at her watch. Twenty minutes until the taxi came. In five more months this high-pressure life would be over, and oh, how glad she'd be! Modelling had been good to her, but only ever as a means to an end.

She stared with dispassionate interest at the face that had looked out from a million magazines, been admired on the world's most noted catwalks, a face almost universally heralded as her generation's most mesmerising.

Not that Perdita had ever succumbed to the extravagant ravings of the hype machine. During the last ten years she'd developed a healthy cynicism. When she began she'd been the trendsetter; her dramatic bone-structure, height of six feet and translucent Celtic skin were touted as the look of the decade, the eight or nine pale golden freckles across her nose providing a piquant contrast to the starkly sculptured, sensuous spareness of her face.

It was the right look at the right time and she owed it to the photographer in Auckland who had taken the first shots for her portfolio.

He'd insisted she pose for a full-face profile wearing the high headdress of Nefertiti, wife of the Pharaoh of Egypt. The contrast between her heavy-lidded, oriental air of serene mystery and her warm northern European colouring had created an enormous stir. That photograph had taken her all the way from New Zealand to the heights of international fame. And she'd achieved 'the Perdita look' as a very nervous seventeen-year-old wearing jeans, a towel around her breasts, and a headdress co-opted from a fancy-dress hire business!

However, her decade was over. Elfin waifs were set to conquer the fashionable world during the next twelve months, and Perdita was going to take her hefty investment portfolio and substantial bank balance and retire thankfully to the obscurity from which she'd come.

Brushing back the flood of barely waving, silky amber hair that was her trademark, she pulled a face at her reflection. Obscurity couldn't come soon enough.

Outside, the New York traffic thundered past in a hail of tooting, jostling, urgent taxi cabs. And the telephone rang.

'Damn,' she muttered in a voice that still held faint traces of a New Zealand accent. It had to be someone she trusted; her number was unlisted. And that meant it was reasonably important. Picking up the receiver, she said crisply, 'Hello?'

'Perdita Gladstone?' There was more than a trace of New Zealand in this masculine voice. It was pure NewZild, broad and unashamed.

The breath died in Perdita's throat. Staring blindly out over Fifth Avenue to the green, interloper's glory of Central Park, she swallowed as one hand curved protectively around the antique Victorian locket—another trademark—which she wore on a thin gold chain around her neck.

'Yes, it is I,' she said hoarsely, giving the simple code she had worked out with him.

For ten years she had been waiting for this, for half that time searching actively. The last occasion Frank had rung he'd said the name she wanted was very close.

'I've got them.' He always tried to sound deadpan as a good private detective should, but there was no hiding the jubilant note in his voice. 'Natalie and Luke Dennison. They live at a little place called Manley up in Northland.'

Shock dimmed the green trees in the park, banished the everpresent throb and hum of the city to a faint, gasping echo. Perdita looked back, down ten years to a place so far removed from this that they might well be on different planets.

She'd known there was an element of risk in what she was doing; she'd had no idea that it would jeopardise everything she had made of her life.

'Are you there? Miss Gladstone? Perdita?' Frank's voice registered a sudden alarm.

'Dennison?' The voice wasn't hers. It croaked rather than breathed, and the cool control was lost to a shaky tremor. 'I'm all right. Dennison,' she repeated on a long, ragged sigh. 'Luke Dennison.'

'Yup. He's a big man in the north—owns a huge cattle and sheep station called Pigeon Hill. He's fairly well known—old money, family came over on the first ships, mixes with the élite, that sort of thing. Prime ministers consult him, and he belongs to a lot of very powerful organisations.'

'I know,' she said, outrage beginning to surface through the numbness.

'You know him?' Frank was curious but she couldn't have answered him then, not if her sanity had depended on it. 'He married Natalie Bennet—another family with old money. She died about eighteen months ago. Cancer.'

Perdita groped desperately for a chair. Shivering, she collapsed into it, clutching the receiver with white-knuckled fingers.

'Died?' she managed to repeat.

'Yup, tough, poor woman. She was only thirty-seven. Luke Dennison was a couple of years younger. They were married when he was twenty-one. His parents were both dead and I suppose he needed a wife.'

'Probably,' Perdita agreed tonelessly. 'I have to go, Frank. Can you send me the details?'

'Yeah. It'll be a big bill, I hope you realise. Usually I don't have much difficulty with these cases even when there's a veto, but this was a humdinger. I had a hell of a time tracking down the information. Files were missing or lost, people didn't know or wouldn't talk, and it turned out to be a real challenge. I'd say that someone did their best to make sure no one was able to trace anything. Still, we got there.' He sounded professionally pleased with himself. 'OK, I'll courier everything off straight away, if you're still sure you trust couriers.'

She would have trusted the mail, or copies of the documents on the fax, but Frank had his idiosyncrasies, and one of them was a passion for security and a vast mistrust of agencies that moved information.

Perhaps he was right; when she had first contacted him he had told her that he didn't do anything illegal and she believed him, but she had a feeling that her ideas of illegal and Frank's possibly didn't coincide. She didn't know how he had got this information, and she wasn't going to ask.

'Thank you,' she said levelly.

'That's OK. Glad to get it done. It was starting to take over my life.' He hung up.

Take over his life? Perdita had been waiting for those names for ten years. And now that she had them, the beginning she had anticipated was turning into something else, a nightmare she didn't know how to deal with.

Eventually, when the dialling tone impinged, she set the receiver down and looked at her watch.

'Oh, *panic*!' she muttered, leaping to her feet. She had no time to think, none to dwell on this news, or even to sort out her emotions. But mingled with the grief and the anger and the bewilderment there was another, one she had never expected to feel: a keen, almost brutal sense of betrayal.

For ten years she had been alone and lost, and for those years Natalie and Luke had been happy. Her hand lingered for a moment on the thin gold locket. Whether they'd known it or not, their happiness had been built on her misery.

Setting her mouth, she forced herself to pick up her bag, weighed down by the usual assortment of necessities and the ever-present book on landscape gardening.

Perdita had always prided herself on her professional outlook, and she wasn't going to let the complete upheaval of her life make her late.

Five more months! They stretched out like an eternity.

'What have I done?' she muttered as she opened the door. 'Oh, what have I done?'

CHAPTER ONE

ELEVEN years—a lifetime ago, the last time she had been to Pigeon Hill—she had walked this road beneath a boiling Antipodean sun, tattered shorts and a T-shirt clinging to coltish limbs, her hair shaded by a Huck Finn hat, jandals on her narrow feet. Then the road had been metalled, and her legs had been white with dust by the time she got to Pigeon Hill, the station named after the looming, bush-clad hill where the large, slow-flying native pigeon flourished.

She certainly had never imagined returning to Pigeon Hill in a car that cost more money than she could have visualised at seventeen; then her sights had been set on a job in a shop, and eventually marriage and children.

If a hotel in Wellington hadn't failed to give Luke Dennison a message, that was probably exactly what would have happened.

Because the hotel staff had failed she was a mature, worldly woman with a famous face and body, and a secure future. She should, Perdita supposed, her full lips compressing with the irony of it, thank that unknown person who hadn't done his or her job properly.

Suddenly realising that she was veering towards the wrong side of the road, she twisted the steering-wheel a little too impatiently. She hadn't driven on the left for some years; it would pay to concentrate on her driving, not what had happened so long ago.

Five letterboxes loomed ahead like a cluster of ragged beehives. Suspended from the top bar of the gate was a neat sign that said Pigeon Hill. Beneath it in smaller letters was painted L.D.E. Dennison. Perdita's stomach clenched.

Breathing deeply, she braked. The car rattled over the cattle stop and along the road winding across a wide green paddock towards a cluster of roofs. The three farm cottages belied their name; sheltered from the southerly winds by the blue, forested hill that was Pukekukupa, they were substantial houses, built for families.

A couple of hundred metres before the first one, the well-kept track divided. Perdita took the fork that led to the homestead. Nestled behind its plantations of trees, all that could be seen of it was the pale orange bulk of the roof.

Her mouth dried with anticipatory dread; she had to fight the temptation to turn around and drive down the road, the three and a half hours back to Auckland, then get on to a jet to take her as far from New Zealand as possible. The seatbelt tightened across her chest as her foot hit the brake.

'Oh, no, you don't,' she muttered fiercely, easing it off.

A tunnel of greenery led into a wide, gravelled fore-court in front of a gracious, two-storeyed wooden house built in the colonial Georgian style that had been fashionable seventy years before. As she pulled up and stopped the engine, moisture trickled disgustingly down Perdita's spine and dampened her palms. Surrepti-tiously wiping her hands on a handkerchief before she got out, she forced air into her deflated lungs.

She knew who waited for her inside the homestead. Over Frank's objections she had written to Luke Dennison a week ago to tell him that she was coming, and why.

'He'll run,' Frank warned.

'Not Luke Dennison.' The idea was laughable.

The private investigator had given her a sharp look, but he hadn't asked the question that was so clearly hov-ering on his tongue. Instead, he'd grunted and said pessimistically, 'Then he'll be waiting at the door with a battery of high-powered solicitors waving writs and a couple of policemen.'

'I'll take that chance.'

Now, looking at the perfectly proportioned house, after all these years still intimidated by its air of formal classicism, she wondered whether Frank had been right. Perhaps she should have simply arrived unannounced.

Sheer, cold willpower got her across to the path, and between low box hedges to the panelled front door with its graceful fanlights. Licking parched lips, she rang the doorbell.

To her astonishment Luke Dennison himself opened the door. Her great, gold-speckled green eyes skidded across his face, recreating the countenance of the man who had haunted her for the last eleven years, ever since that last visit to Pigeon Hill.

Four inches taller than Perdita, lean and lithe, perfectly proportioned, his rangy frame was made impressive by the hard muscles of physical labour. He blocked the doorway, watching her with a predator's frightening, disciplined concentration. Neither the eyes that searched her face, eyes the colour and consistency of aquamarines, nor a beautifully cut mouth, softened the angles of his striking, unhandsome face. A straight blade of a nose gave him an air of patrician arrogance.

Dennisons had lived in this place for over a hundred years, lords of all they surveyed, and it showed.

'Hello, Luke,' Perdita said, her tone remote and rigidly controlled.

'Perdita.' Deep and textured to the edge of roughness, he had the kind of voice that could stroke indolently through a woman's defences. However, there was no note of lazy sensuality in it now. Like hers, it was totally lacking in expression, as invulnerable as the compellingly hewn bone-structure of his face, as devoid of emotion as the icy, crystalline eyes. 'Come in.'

Comprehension hit her like a blow as soon as she stepped through the door. *The house was empty*.

The mixture of fear and anticipation that had boosted her for the last five months drained away, leaving her limp with sour reaction, but unsurprised. After all, she hadn't expected it to be easy. Long lashes veiled her eyes, giving her a sultry, enigmatic look.

'The office, I think,' he said, standing back so that she could precede him down the passage and into an expansive room where the latest in computer technology blended in odd harmony with kauri bookshelves and the rich colours, muted by time, of a Persian carpet.

Just inside the door Perdita stopped, regarding the man in front of her with relentless eyes. 'Where are they?' she said with sudden, betraying anxiety.

'Would you like a drink?' he asked, walking across to a cabinet. Instead of the careful gait of most big men he moved with an economical, animal grace that was peculiarly his.

'No, thank you. Where are they?' In spite of herself her voice trembled.

'Sit down.'

She lowered herself into the wing chair, the last traces of nervousness replaced by a resentment that heated her skin and eyes. Although she expected him to loom over her, try to intimidate her with height and the blunt threat of his male strength and power, he too sat down, his pale eyes fixed on her face in a scrutiny that was controlled and ironic.

'I've seen your photograph hundreds of times,' he remarked, an undernote of sarcasm permeating the words, 'and imagined that it was all done with make-up, but I was wrong. You are exquisitely beautiful.'

'My looks are not important,' she said, her voice held level by willpower. He was trying to make her angry—and succeeding only too well. But a fit of temper would compromise her self-command, and he'd take advantage of any weakness. She met his gaze with her own. 'Where are the children?'

His hands were clasped on the desk in the traditional attitude of power. 'Did you really believe they'd be here?' he asked deliberately. 'You must think I'm extraordinarily trusting.'

'It seems that I'm the trusting one.' As she spoke she got to her feet and headed for the door.

'Where do you think you're going?'

'Where does it look as though I'm going? I'm leaving,' she said, relieved that she could sound so unemotional. 'I don't want to socialise. The only reason I'm here was to see the children.'

'Come back and sit down,' he ordered.

Shoulders stiff, she turned reluctantly. 'Why?'

'Because we need to talk.' When she didn't move he leaned back in the chair, narrowed eyes holding hers. 'Common sense should tell you that I'm not going to let you just burst into their life.'

He was right. They did need to talk. She nodded slowly, and walked to the chair, sitting down with a guarded expression that gave, she hoped, nothing away.

'First of all,' he said without inflection, 'why did you suddenly decide after all this time that you want to meet them?'

'It was no *sudden* decision.' She hid a swift flare of anger with precisely chosen words. Did he think she'd come back on a whim? 'I've always wanted to know how they are, but until a few months ago I couldn't find out who had adopted them.' She smiled humourlessly, repressing memories of the outrage she had experienced then, the pain and the strange, weakening exultation. 'Now that I know, I want to see them.'

'If you can convince me that you won't upset them,' he said collectedly, 'then you may see them.'

Her green glance mocked him. 'Really? You'll excuse the faint note of disbelief, I'm sure. Somehow I got the distinct impression that you'd have been more than happy if your children's birth mother had never turned up. You certainly covered your tracks well. In spite of the new laws, it's taken me five years to find out who adopted my daughters. You have a lot of power, Luke.'

'And I'll use it,' he said with a soft menace that dragged the hairs on her skin upright in a primitive, involuntary reaction, 'to stop anyone from hurting my children.'

'I don't want to hurt them.' If she wanted to hurt anyone it was him. 'I just need to see that they're happy.'

Dark brows snapped together. 'Why shouldn't they be happy?' he demanded. 'They're loved and cared for.'

'I need to be sure of that.' She closed her eyes for a second. 'They are *my* daughters as well as yours. I didn't abandon them, you know. I'd have kept them if I could.'

He didn't move, didn't react in any way, yet somehow she sensed that her frank plea had struck home. She leaned forward. 'It doesn't have to be here,' she said quietly. 'We could meet somewhere in a park. I just want to talk to them. I won't tell them who I am.'

'And if you think they're unhappy?' he asked with disbelieving curtness. 'What will you do then?'

'I don't know. But—I'm not unreasonable, Luke. You're their father, you've had them since they were a week old, and I'm not going to interfere unless I think the situation warrants it.' An aching smile curved her wide, lush mouth. 'I don't expect it to. I just want to see them.'

He said heavily, 'I suppose your private detective told you that Natalie is dead.'

Perdita's lashes quivered. 'Yes.'

She knew how much Luke had loved his wife, knew that her death must have been shattering to them all. As it had been to her.

In the older woman, her mother's cousin, the young, emotionally neglected Perdita had found the love and consideration she had never been able to elicit from her own mother. Luke's wife had loved her and valued her, and because Natalie was gracious and charming and affectionate, Perdita had responded with a child's unquestioning gratitude. At eleven, newly come to Pigeon Hill, she had been struck up by Natalie's conviction that life was perfectible—it merely needed work—and vowed to grow up as much like Natalie as she could. It still struck her as an excellent ambition, although she had long given up believing that she could ever resemble her cousin. Such people were born, not made.

'I'm so sorry,' she said now, her voice uneven in spite of her attempt to steady it. 'Oh, Luke, I am so sorry.'

He looked at her. 'I really believe you are,' he said harshly.

'Of course I am! I loved her.' Perdita swallowed, but nervous tension had her well and truly in its grip. Tears pearled through her fingers as she pressed them to her eyes, slid down her hands. She sniffed, and groped in her bag.

'Here,' Luke said, his voice strained.

A soft handkerchief was thrust into her hand. Turning away from him she blew her nose and swallowed hard. She couldn't afford to give in to her emotions, it made her too vulnerable.

Wiping her eyes, she said thickly, 'How did the girls take it?'

'As you'd expect.' He spoke with barely caged impatience. 'They were shattered, but they've come through it fairly well. However, there's been enough turmoil in their lives. I don't want them upset again.'

'All I'm interested in is their happiness. Do they know they're adopted?'

'Of course they do.' He shrugged. 'Natalie insisted.'

Being Natalie, she would have done everything right. Everything but stay alive.

'Did Natalie know they were my daughters?' she asked, unable to stop herself. Ever since she had read in Frank's dossier that her daughters' names were Olivia and Rosalind she had wondered whether Natalie and Luke had somehow discovered that she was their mother.

However, common sense told her it was just that Natalie liked Shakespearian names; she had always admired Perdita, saying once that when she had daughters she could do worse than search through his plays.

Now Perdita waited, holding her breath, shadowed eyes searching Luke's hard-boned, uncompromising face with something like anguish, but his studied composure was so absolute that nothing could have broken through it.

'No,' he said deliberately, 'and neither did I. All details of their parentage were kept quiet, although we were given character traits and intelligence, a few physical characteristics, things like that.' In a voice that held derision he finished, 'I was pleased the father was so like me.'

Her relief startled her, lowering her guard enough for her to blurt, 'Didn't you even wonder?'

His mouth twisted. 'I didn't know you were pregnant. Your mother certainly wasn't telling anyone.'

Perdita opened her mouth to tell him that Natalie had known, she had visited her in the nursing home, but he forestalled her ruthlessly. 'Not that it matters. Even if you can prove that you are their birth mother, Perdita, you have no legal claim to the children.'

'I know that. I accept it. Is it so difficult to believe that I simply want to see them, to reassure myself that they're happy?'

He said forcefully, 'I don't think you'd be a good influence.'

Perdita's head lifted sharply, the bell of heavy hair falling across her neck in a silken swathe. For a moment she was speechless, scanning his face to see whether he could possibly be joking. He wasn't. He meant every word he said. Evenly, almost lightly, she asked, 'Why is that?'

'The life you've led these past ten years.' He waited for her answer, and when she didn't speak said with cold-blooded austerity, 'My daughters are only ten, Perdita.

You've spent those ten years in the fast lane, living with a variety of lovers, leading an infinitely more sophisticated life than anything New Zealand can offer. I'd be at fault as a father if I allowed you the chance to impose your *demi-mondaine* manners and morals on them.'

Her face a mask of scorn, she got to her feet and confronted him fearlessly. 'What a smug, sanctimonious prig you are, Luke. I don't understand how Natalie could love you. Listen to me, and don't forget it, because I'm not going to say it again. *I intend to see my children.* If necessary I'll stay in Manley until they come back from wherever you've hidden them, and then sneak around to see them. I gave you the chance of doing it properly, but I *will* see them, whether you want me to or not.'

Ignoring his sharply indrawn breath, she turned towards the door, but before she had reached it he was barring the way, his face set in lines of contempt and anger, aquamarine eyes blazing with frigid fire.

'Let me past,' she said between her teeth.

'Not until I've had my say,' he returned dangerously. 'Listen to *me*, Perdita, and for once think of someone other than yourself. Those girls have just come through a traumatic time. They don't need any more pain. I swear, if you hurt them, confuse them or upset them, I'll make you suffer so much that you'll wish to God you'd never been born.'

She had to tilt her head back to look up into his face. Sheer fury turned her eyes to smoky pools, her voice to a molten purr. 'Then you'd better come with them when I see them,' she said softly, 'so that you can monitor my behaviour. *Because I am going to see them.*'

He swore. Perdita had learned to ignore swearing, but she flinched at the naked hatred in his voice. 'You little bitch,' he said slowly. 'I thought I was rid of you—why the hell did you have to come back?'

An emotion Perdita thought had died forever struggled in painful rebirth deep in some walled-off portion of her heart.

'You must have known I would, as soon as I found out where the girls were.'

'I didn't know you were their mother until I got your letter three days ago.' His eyes were opaque and hard and lethal. 'We were told their mother had gone overseas and wouldn't be coming back.'

'Whoever told you that was wrong. I'm like Nemesis,' she said silkily. 'I never give up. Now, get out of my way.'

He stepped back as though the mere touch of her would contaminate him. 'I'll serve you with a non-molestation order,' he threatened.

'I'll go to the media,' she countered sweetly. 'It would make good headlines, wouldn't it? Especially if the British tabloids got hold of it. I'm quite famous, you know—they'd enjoy a good juicy scandal like that.'

He seemed to grow a further six inches. The implacable resistance she sensed in him was converted into a cold, concentrated fury. 'You wouldn't dare,' he said in an almost soundless voice.

She couldn't allow herself to be intimidated so completely. 'Are you prepared to bet on that?' she asked. 'After all, anyone with my *morals and manners* has to be untrustworthy by definition.'

His hands slid around her throat. Fear slithered on evil cats' feet through Perdita's body, throbbed in the pulse beneath his fingers, chilled the anger in her veins to elemental ice. She saw pitiless determination in the gaze that fixed on to her mouth, smelt the faint, unmistakable scent of male, aroused and relentless.

Once before Luke Dennison had slipped the leash of his control to reveal the primal male to her. Now she saw it again, and as had happened that last time, an elemental terror turned her bones to liquid.

'I've already warned you,' he said quietly, a thumb coming to rest over the busy betrayer in her throat. 'You've pushed as far as you're going to, Perdita. Any more, and you'd better be ready for retaliation.'

Common sense told her that there was nothing he could do to her. This was New Zealand, after all.

Instinct knew otherwise.

Yet she didn't flinch, even though she felt the colour drain from her skin. 'Stop trying to frighten me,' she said, green eyes as cold as his, and every bit as determined. 'None of this drama is necessary, Luke. If you let me meet the children I'll go on my way, and you won't need to be bothered by me any more.'

'I don't want you anywhere near them,' he said, levering her chin upwards to an unnatural angle that stretched her throat towards the frail boundary between discomfort and pain.

His immediate, total rejection scored across her heart like the cruellest of whips. She lowered her lashes so that all she could see of his face was the angular line of his jaw, as obdurate as his character, tough and uncompromising. She should have expected this; she, of all people, knew how hard he could be.

'You can't stop me,' she said, hating the tremor in her voice, trying to summon courage from some deep inner reserve. 'Be sensible, Luke. You can't keep them imprisoned forever, and there's no way you can run me out of town this time.'

'Go on,' he said when she fell silent.

'That's all. I'm going to see them.'

'Damn you,' he muttered. 'I've been haunted by you for bloody years—you must have known that coming back here would put us all in an intolerable situation!'

Then he kissed her.

The fierce possession of his mouth summoned a fire that marked her soul. Searing through the debris and accretions of the past eleven years, it stripped every bit of studied worldliness from her to cast her back into the adolescent turmoil of her first crush, the year she had turned seventeen.

Natalie had given her a watch and a new wardrobe to mark her status as an adult, and, dressed in the clothes his wife had bought for her, Perdita had fallen in love with Luke, helpless in the grip of a blind, unrequited passion.

That same passion, so newly reawakened, thrummed through her now with an intensity she didn't even try to resist. She melted, her mouth softening, yielding, opening to his like a flower to the sun. Drumbeats pulsed through her in a rhythm of desire. Shivering, she was suffused with heat.

Luke ground his mouth on to hers, but almost immediately the quality of the kiss changed, transformed into seduction pure and simple, as nakedly sexual as the embrace that clamped her hips against his, as the utterly masculine promise that fitted so snugly between the notch in her legs.

Perdita drowned in sensation, sanity and reason wrecked by a flood of carnality.

And then he thrust her from him and said jaggedly, 'Get the hell out of here, you lying, promiscuous little slut. I don't ever want to see you again.'

Perdita stared at him from beneath weighted eyelids. Her mouth was tender, slightly too big for its contours, and she was drunk on the taste of him, the scent of him, the feel of him.

Half her brain was shrieking foul, and the other half was cursing because she'd allowed herself to trip into the oldest snare in the world, but below these manifestations of logic lurked a consuming, primitive satisfaction.

'You're not going to get rid of me so easily,' she said, her voice husky and sensual. 'Like it or not, Luke, you can't bludgeon me with your money and your power. I mean to see those girls, and there is no way you can watch them so strictly that I won't.'

His hands were shaking. She watched with awed fascination as he reimposed control, a fascination that had a basis of fear, because she knew what he wanted to do with them.

'Yes,' he said when he saw her glance at them, 'you should be afraid. Get out of here, Perdita, before I do something you might regret.'

'I'm staying at the Dunromin motel in Manley,' she told him, and turned and walked away from him through the big, gracious, empty house, out into the sunlight. Constrained by the silk scarf bound around her head, her temples throbbed painfully. She put up a long-fingered hand to draw it off, and with a slow movement shook the flood of hair back.

Tension still ached through her, but she wasn't going to stretch herself free of it here, where he might be watching. She knew why he had kissed her; it was an unsubtle punishment because she was alive and Natalie was dead. He hadn't been able to hit back at fate, or cry his despair at the moon, so he had done what men had done to women ever since the world began: used his superior strength and turned anger into sexuality.

She was, she realised with a strange sort of detachment, still shuddering inside, but at least the worst was over. She had seen him. Now all she had to do was find the children.

This voyage into the past had assumed all the qualities of a search for the holy grail. When she saw the children she would know, she was sure, whether they were happy or not.

And if they were happy, that would be it. She'd get into the car and drive away...

Although, sooner or later natural curiosity would drive them to search for their birth mother. Surely, some tempter whispered, that discovery would be less traumatic if she were not a complete stranger. Of course she would never be a substitute for Natalie, but she might make some small place for herself in her children's lives.

Luke had no right to keep her away from her children. Apart from anything else, he'd behaved very badly, insulting her, manhandling her, kissing her...

The idea was far too enticing. Even as she reminded herself sternly that she had promised Luke she wouldn't interfere, she knew she was going to consult a lawyer.

Back at the motel she made herself a cup of tea and sat down. Her hand came to rest on the locket around her neck. With a sudden, swift movement she flicked through her purse and found the one photograph she had of her children, a coloured snap one of the nurses had taken of them when they were a week old.

The young Perdita sat stiffly, holding the two babies with such care that she looked terrified, staring straight at the camera. They were both girls, one thirty minutes older than the other, but even then it had been obvious that they were not identical. She had called them Tara and Melissa.

They were asleep; she had crept into the nursery and taken them outside for the photograph. Her eyes looked glazed because she had been fighting back tears. The next day she had left the nursing home, and the couple who had adopted her children had come and taken them away.

How would she have felt if she had known they were Natalie, whom she loved with the hero-worship of a neglected child, and Luke?

It was better that she hadn't known. It would never have worked. She'd been far too young to cope with the situation.

She wasn't, she thought wryly, coping too well with it now, and it was five months since Frank's call.

The colours in the photograph had faded, but she could remember everything about her children, even their faint scent of baby powder and milk and innocence. A resurgence of the old pain gnawed at her. She had never forgotten, not a thing.

And Luke Dennison was not going to stand in her way. He had money and power, but she had money too, and the power of her threat. Although she hadn't any intention of contacting the media—she knew how badly hurt its victims could be—it was a threat she could hold over his head.

She was going to see her daughters.

Refusing to think of the way he had kissed her, the angry manifestation of his power used to intimidate her, she drank the cup of tea before ringing an Auckland number.

Frank whistled when she told him what she wanted him to do. 'I told you not to tell him. You can't trust people when it comes to children. Any ideas?'

'Try Mrs Bennet, Mrs Philip Bennet. She used to live in Epsom—I'm almost certain it was Owens Road. She's the grandmother. Oh, and can you give me the name and address of that solicitor you were recommending—the one who specialises in family law.'

'Yup.' He didn't say again that he'd told her so, but she heard it in the monosyllable.

She scribbled down the name and address he gave her, said goodbye and hung up, then turned to look around her. The room was small and sparsely furnished in motel style, with furniture that didn't fit her long legs and body. The rush of adrenalin that had sustained her so far faded slowly, leaving her melancholy and thoughtful.

Setting her mouth, she went out into the street and called into the florist's shop. They weren't busy so the woman made her a posy of cottage flowers while she waited, looking at her curiously when she thought she was unobserved.

After Perdita had paid for them she said in a rush, 'You know, you look awfully like that model—the Adventurous Woman.'

Perdita gave her a warm smile. 'I'm retired, now,' she said.

The woman's eyes widened. 'You came from around here, didn't you?'

'I used to spend holidays here with my cousin.'

'Mrs Dennison at Pigeon Hill.' She sighed. 'That was a tragedy. She was a lovely lady.'

'Yes.'

'Oh, well, you must be noticing quite a few changes in the last ten years.'

Perdita smiled again. 'Quite a few. The place has grown.'

'Are you planning on living here?'

Until that moment the thought had never occurred to Perdita. She said vaguely, 'No, I don't think so,' but as she walked out of the shop the idea took root and on the way down the hill to the cemetery it flourished. Nothing would give her greater pleasure than to live close to her daughters.

But would it be fair to them?

And how would Luke deal with that? At the thought of his reaction her skin prickled. He was a bad enemy.

The little graveyard had served the district well for over a hundred years. Perdita walked across newly mown grass sheltered by the huge old puriri and totara trees that made a dense barrier around the perimeter. It was very quiet and still.

Natalie's headstone was plain and austere. With wet eyes Perdita read that she was the beloved wife of Luke, loved mother of Olivia and Rosalind, aged thirty-seven years.

Stooping, Perdita put her flowers with the others there. Death was so final, so impersonally unfair, when it carried off those who were young and good and happy.

She turned away, only then seeing through the sparkle of tears the tall, powerful figure of the man who had made Natalie so happy. Damn, she thought, suddenly exhausted by emotion. Why did he have to come here now?

Head held high, chin tilted, she waited beside the grave. He'd see the results of her grief, but she wasn't ashamed of it.

His face was set in lines of harsh restraint. 'What the hell are you doing here?'

She said, 'I brought flowers.'

He closed his eyes as though she couldn't have said anything more painful. On a note of bitterness she finished, 'I loved her too, Luke.'

'Yes, I know,' he said heavily, looking down at the bunch of cottagey flowers, bright cornflowers and spray carnations in a froth of white gypsophila.

'She was so kind to me,' Perdita said.

He jerked his head away but she saw the flash of naked emotion in his pale eyes. Gripped by compassion, she touched his arm. He had rolled up his sleeves, so her fingers were pale and slender against the tanned forearm with its light dusting of hair. The heat of his skin burned through barriers she hadn't been aware of. Something moved deeply inside her. Snatching her fingers away, she had to resist the temptation to cool them in her mouth.

Hastily she went on, 'She taught me how to dress and how to behave, that I wasn't strange because I liked to read. In a funny sort of way she gave me my career. If she hadn't taken me to Clive's that Christmas to buy my clothes he wouldn't have recommended me to the model agency. My life would have been as narrow and circumscribed as my mother's. Natalie gave me everything, and she did it with such grace and empathy. She never made me feel that I was a gawky nothing.'

'She groomed you to take her place,' Luke said bitterly. 'I wonder what she'd have thought of that.'

His words drove every vestige of colour from her face. Instinctively she stepped back, casting a swift, horrified glance at the mute grave.

His mouth curled into a mirthless, wolfish smile. 'It's all right,' he said. 'She can't hear you. She'll never know that you betrayed her love by seducing her husband. She'll never know that the children she adopted and loved so much were yours and mine. She's dead, Perdita, and you and I are left to wonder just what would have happened if she hadn't died. Because you'd have come back just the same, wouldn't you?'

Perdita's lips trembled. 'Yes.'

'And created even more damage than you did when you crawled into my bed that night.'

She shook her head, but he went on relentlessly, 'Why did you do it?'

'I told you. I was asleep when you came to bed. I didn't expect you home that night,' she said indistinctly.

The sun summoned auburn fire from his hair. His eyes were as cold as his laugh, as completely lacking in amusement.

'Even though it was the bed Natalie and I slept in every night?' He let the pause linger for endless moments, then brought it to an end by saying smoothly, 'I find that very difficult to believe.'

She had slept in their bed because Luke was due back from three days spent in Wellington, and Natalie had decided to go halfway to Auckland to meet him at the house of friends.

'He'll be tired after three days' arguing with the government,' she'd said. 'I'll meet him at the Gardiners', and we'll stay there, then come back tomorrow after he's had a good night's rest. You won't mind staying here, will you?'

Of course Perdita didn't mind.

'Just in case you're nervous, why don't you sleep in our room?' Natalie suggested. 'The phone's right by the bed. Oh, and if you find it difficult to sleep in a strange bed my sleeping pills will be in the drawer. They're quite harmless. They don't knock you out, they're more like calming pills than sleeping pills, really.'

'I won't need them,' Perdita said.

Natalie hugged her. 'What it is to be young and able to sleep on the head of a pin! I'll leave one there just the same. Right, now that that's organised, I'll go and ring the hotel so he knows about the change of plans.'

But the anonymous someone in Luke's hotel in Wellington hadn't handed on the message, and Luke had driven all the way home, to find Perdita, slightly drugged with the pill because lying in Luke's bed had given her too much of a secret, forbidden thrill, asleep in the innocent abandon of childhood. She hadn't heard him come in, hadn't realised until she woke in his arms that he had thought she was Natalie. And by then she had been unable to think...

But she couldn't tell him that now. After it happened she had tried to explain, and he had refused to believe her, cursing her for stealing something that had been Natalie's, exiling her to Auckland and her mother, who didn't want her and had never forgiven her for driving her father away.

'It's a bit late to be putting flowers on her grave,' Luke said curtly. 'You repaid Natalie by betraying her.'

The words were like fiery arrows, tearing Perdita's composure to shreds. Stung, still racked by guilt, she flung back, 'As you did!'

'Oh, yes,' he said quietly. 'You don't have to try to make me feel guilty, Perdita. I've never been free of it since that night.'

'It wasn't your fault you thought I was Natalie,' she said. It had been Natalie he'd held in his arms, Natalie who was the recipient of his savage tenderness, Natalie...

'That's no excuse,' he returned with raw self-contempt.

There was no answer to that. It was no excuse, and neither was the fact that she hadn't been intent on seduction that night. She could have kicked and screamed and forced him to realise that she wasn't Natalie, but when she woke it was too late—her sleeping body had been seduced by his practised caresses, and she had yielded without protest, without making a sound.

He said abruptly, 'You can see the children.'

She turned a radiant face to him, but before she could speak he went on, 'On one condition. I want you to sign a document saying that you won't tell them who you are, and that you have no claim to them.'

Perdita hesitated and he said evenly, 'No document, no visit.'

She understood his caution. Nodding, she agreed, 'Yes, all right.'

'Right. Be at the solicitor's office at four this afternoon.'

CHAPTER TWO

PRECISELY at that time Perdita presented herself at the solicitor's office. She had already contacted the expert in family law in Auckland, and been warned to sign nothing that might prejudice her chances of access to the girls.

Actually, he had suggested very strongly that she forward any documents to him for scrutiny, but Perdita had almost made up her mind to sign. She didn't want to take her daughters away from the only home they had known; she merely wanted to make sure that they were happy.

And perhaps when Luke realised that she wasn't a bad influence he would allow her to get to know them properly. Although his accusation still rankled, there was, she had to admit, some cause for it. Gossip columnists had had a field day with one or two of her supposed lovers.

The legal document, short and to the point, was waiting for her. She agreed not to tell the children that she was their birth mother, and she agreed that this meeting constituted no claim to further access or custody.

That seemed fair enough. Ignoring the elderly solicitor's somewhat censorious attitude, she signed, then got gracefully to her feet.

He said, 'I would urge you to think of the welfare of these children, Ms Gladstone.'

She gave him a cool, remote glance. He had come out to Pigeon Hill occasionally to parties, seeming older then to a teenaged girl than he did now. Their slight acquaintanceship gave him no right to imagine that he could influence her. He, and everyone else who had known her then, would have to realise that the child who used to stay at Pigeon Hill during the holidays, the recipient of her cousin's charity, had grown up.

'I don't think this is any of your business. Goodbye,' she said calmly, and walked across the room, ignoring the faint sputtering from behind her.

She had just reached the door when the telephone rang. Stepping through, she closed the door behind her, only to re-open it swiftly when her name was called from inside the room.

'Yes?' she asked aloofly.

He put the receiver down. 'That was Luke,' he said with stiff precision. 'He wants to see you out at Pigeon Hill. Now.'

Her brows shot up. 'Thank you,' she said.

As she turned to go once more he said, 'Take some advice from an old man, Perdita. Luke can be ruthless, especially where those children are concerned. They were all that kept him sane when Natalie died. He is intensely protective of them.'

A tight smile barely moved her mouth. 'Thank you,' she said sweetly, and left.

Whether or not he meant it kindly, she preferred to treat it as such. Not that he needed to tell her anything about Luke Dennison. She knew all about him, including the fact that he was a superbly tender lover.

But she, too, could be ruthless. First Natalie, then her life as a model, had taught her that she had to stand up for herself, fight for what she wanted and believed in.

And there was nothing she wanted more than to see her children.

What did his summons to the station mean? Were the girls there? Her heart thudded as she got into her car and set it in motion, concentrating on keeping to the left. Where there was other traffic it was simple, but once she got on to the no-exit road to Pigeon Hill she found her attention wavering, and a couple of times had to head back on to the correct side.

As before, Luke met her at the door, his angular face without expression. 'They're in the morning-room,' he said.

Now that the ambition that had sustained her for ten long years was about to be realised, Perdita found she didn't dare move. Instead, she stared at him as though she had never seen a man before. His image wavered and blurred. Colour leached from her skin as the floor tilted beneath her feet.

'Perdita!' he said sharply.

Shivering, she was swept up in his arms and carried across the hall and into another room. He put her down on a sofa and ordered, 'Don't move. I'll get you some brandy.'

Perdita closed her eyes. Almost immediately she heard whispering, and lifted heavy lashes to see the two girls coming across the room to her.

She'd always known they weren't identical; what she hadn't expected was for them to be quite so different.

One was a willowy creature with long limbs and a face whose bones had come straight from her mother, whereas her sister was small and sleek and—seeking the right word to describe her, Perdita could only find *merry*. Her eyes twinkled, she smiled with heart-lifting brightness, and her expression was alert and alive and vital, a contrast to the grave thoughtfulness of the other girl. The taller of the two had blue eyes whereas the other's, Perdita was shaken to see, were the same green as hers; both had hair that was gloriously, unashamedly red, but the taller had straight, shoulder-length locks and the shorter's curled around her piquant face.

'Hello,' Perdita said, smiling at them. Her heart clattered noisily, almost suffocating her. The last time she had seen them they had been seven days old, and she had been numb with despair, her throat raw from weeping. Something of the same agony of spirit racked her now, desolation and a sense of bitter deprivation,

of loneliness so intense she'd had to repress it to be able
to bear it.

'Hello,' they chorused, then looked at each other, said,
'Tennyson,' and linked little fingers, shutting their eyes
as they made a wish.

The age-old ritual soothed something in Perdita's
heart. She said, 'I hope your wish comes true.'

'So do we,' the shorter one said cheekily. She looked
Perdita over with open interest and said, 'Don't you feel
well?'

'No, I——'

'She almost fell at my feet.' Luke appeared with a small
glass of brandy. 'Here, drink it down,' he said.

'I feel much better already.'

'Drink it.'

She opened her mouth and the girls giggled. 'You'd
better do what he says,' the shorter advised. 'Mummy
used to say when he gets that note in his voice he means
to be obeyed.'

Perdita knew their names, even knew that the taller
one was Olivia and the shorter Rosalind, but until Luke
introduced them with the same austere courtesy he used
for adult women she had always thought of them as Tara
and Melissa. By the time she had adjusted to this they
were all sitting down and the girls were looking at her
with interest and a certain astonishment.

'I know who you are,' Rosalind said eagerly. 'You're
a model, aren't you? You're the Adventurous Woman.'

A famous, old-established firm of cosmetic makers
had rejuvenated its rather stuffy image with an advertising campaign that had aroused an enormous amount
of interest. The Adventurous Woman concept had
boosted sales to delirious, unexpected heights, doing
wonders for the bank balances of the company, the advertising agency and Perdita.

'I used to be,' she said, setting the barely tasted brandy
down on the small side table. 'Not any more. I'm retired.'

She didn't look at Luke but she felt his keen attention; her skin tightened.

Rosalind laughed. 'You look too young to be retired. Didn't you like being a model?'

'Some of it was fun,' Perdita admitted. 'But a lot of it is pretty boring, just flicking your head around for photographers. And it was very hard work. Still, I didn't go to university and get qualifications, so I had to take what I could get.'

They had Natalie's exquisite manners. They talked freely and pleasantly, of their grandmother, of school, they asked questions about places she had been to, and Perdita found herself telling funny little anecdotes, absurdly thrilled when they laughed and commented. Occasionally she had to prompt them, but they were infinitely more confident than she had been at the same age.

Although afraid to let any emotions other than the most superficial pleasure in their company show through, Perdita gave herself up to an exquisite heartache.

After an hour Luke intervened smoothly, and she found herself being escorted to the door. The girls wanted to come too, but when Luke refused they gave in without demur, saying their farewells with a poised charm that was so like their dead mother that Perdita had to look away in case they saw the tears in her eyes.

He walked down the path with her, waiting until they got to the car before saying abruptly, 'I hope you're satisfied.'

Nodding, face averted, she put out a hand to open the door.

'And I have your promise that you won't contact them in any way?'

Again her head moved.

He said on a steely note, 'Look at me, Perdita,' and his hand caught her chin and tilted her face.

Through the mist of her tears the forceful, uncompromising contours of his face were indistinct, only the pale glitter of his eyes burning clear and brilliant.

For a moment time froze. Then she gave a great sob, and he said furiously, 'God, Perdita, don't——'

'I'm sorry,' she wept. 'It's nothing. I'll be all right soon.'

'I can't let you go like that.' But he released her.

His reluctance enveloped her, palpable and disabling. Shivering, she tried to open the door of the car.

'You can't drive in that state,' he said curtly.

She let the handle go to scrabble for a handkerchief, finally found the one that lurked in the bottom of her bag, and blew her nose. Fresh tears welled up, but she fought them back. She had to get out of here before she really lost control and started to bellow like a kid with a lost toy.

'Goodbye,' she said thickly, and this time she managed to drag the door open and get in. Luke said something but she shook her head and started the engine and took off along the drive, her hands gripping the wheel as though it was the only stable thing in her life. Just before the trees cut off the house her eyes flicked to the rear vision mirror; she registered that he hadn't moved, and was still looking after her like a tall, angry god of olden times.

She held out until she got back to the motel and there, casting herself on to the green and brown and orange sunflowers of the duvet, she wept. Eventually, when her head was aching and her throat raw, the preceding almost sleepless weeks finally caught up with her; from tears she slid straight to unconsciousness.

Some time later she woke with a jolt to the sound of knocking and a voice calling her name with an urgency that had her on her feet and running across to the door.

Luke stood outside; she realised with a shock that it was getting dark, so she must have been asleep for several hours.

'What is it?' she demanded, her voice shaky, clutching the arm that was lifted to knock again on the door. 'The girls——?'

'No, they're fine. I came to make sure you were all right.'

Slowly her hands relaxed and fell to her side. 'Of course I'm all right,' she said in a voice still husky from weeping.

Someone came to the motel office door and peered out at them. Instantly Luke pushed her inside and followed, looking around the room with something like distaste.

'No, don't put the light on,' he commanded as her hand went towards the switch.

She understood immediately. 'Guarding your reputation?' she asked huskily, and went over to the windows to pull the curtains. 'Won't they recognise your car?'

He said shortly, 'I'm sorry, it was a stupid thing to say.'

She knew why he'd said it. Small towns were a hotbed of gossip, especially if you were Luke Dennison, and he hadn't wanted word to get back to the wife who had been dead for eighteen months. Like Perdita, he suffered from a guilt that could never be absolved because it could never be confessed.

If anything was needed to convince her that his heart was buried with Natalie, it was that swift, unconscious remark.

'It's probably wisest,' she said, trying not to let anything but self-possession appear in her tone. Carefully avoiding his eyes, she flicked the light switch down. 'The Manley gossips would have a field day.'

'What are your plans now?' he asked. He stood still in the middle of the small, unmemorable room, taking up most of the space.

She looked at him with studied composure. 'I don't really know,' she said. The florist's remark flashed into her mind, followed by an imp of malice that persuaded her to add, 'I might decide to settle here.'

Although he was so big, the lean muscle on his frame stopped him from being bulky, so the swift, overwhelming sensation of being loomed over was sharp and intimidating. He wasn't blocking any light from her, yet the room was suddenly darker and colder.

Then a straight black brow rose and something like derision glinted through his lashes. 'Here? Out of your milieu, isn't it? You're too expensive, too sophisticated to settle in a one-horse town like Manley. There's no Gerard Defarge, no Kurt Maxwell, no Whoever-he-was Albemarle here, no nightclubs or casinos or chic, expensive fashion boutiques. You'd die of boredom.'

She froze, lifting incredulous eyes to meet his sardonic gaze.

'Somehow,' she said, hiding the quick, unbidden flicker of fear with her most dismissive voice, 'I didn't see you as an avid reader of gossip columns.'

'Natalie used to read them out to me,' he said. 'She thought I'd be interested.'

Natalie would have been interested. It was part of her charm, that absorption in everyone she met. When Natalie spoke to you, it was as though for her you were the only person in the world at that moment.

'But you weren't,' Perdita said coolly.

His mouth hardened. 'I wondered whether it was your abrupt introduction to sex that had set you on that path.'

She looked warily at him. For years, until Frank's revelations of five months ago, she had thought of him as a Sir Galahad, a man who had made a mistake and would spend the rest of his life paying for it, a noble man who loved his wife beyond all reckoning.

Now she didn't know. The missing files and great gaps in the adoption record had made her suspicious.

That first, keenly anticipated meeting with her daughters over, she could think of other things. Someone had tried to make sure she never found her children.

Luke was capable of doing such a thing if he considered that it would protect his children or his wife.

Of course, that would mean that he had known all along that the girls were his. Had the biographical details of the parents made him wonder? Had he lived a lie for ten years?

'I really don't remember much of that first time; I was asleep during most of it.' With the memory of his kiss still imprinted in her cells, she let her anger with herself for falling prey once more to her adolescent desires lead her into continuing acidly, 'Sorry, I'm sure you're an expert lover, but you didn't register. And don't worry about ruining my young life and directing me onto the primrose path. I didn't blame you then, and I don't now. I'm a perfectly normal woman with perfectly normal needs, and I satisfy them in perfectly normal ways.'

And put that in your pipe and smoke it, she thought fiercely, ashamed because she was lying to him. Oh, there had been one other man, but their affair had faded because she couldn't return his passion.

The skin over Luke's jaw tightened. Something savage and untamed leapt into his eyes, was almost brought under control.

'I'm glad to hear it,' he said brusquely. 'But you won't find glamorous, rich men here in Manley.'

'And you don't want me anywhere near the children,' she said, not trying to hide the irony in her smile.

He shrugged. 'Do you blame me for looking after their interests?' Astonishingly, he put up a hand and touched the dried tear track on her cheek.

Mesmerised by the gentleness of his touch, Perdita stared at him. His eyes gleamed, slivers of pure colour beneath half-closed lids, and his mouth was set in a thin, straight line. Her heartbeat suddenly increased speed. She had to force herself to step backwards, away from the swift, sharp lance of sensation.

'Of course I don't,' she said, aware that he was manipulating her, yet unable to resent it. She too would protect her children to the utmost of her ability. 'But I don't want to hurt them, or upset them, or even make them wonder who I am. I gather that Natalie didn't mention me to them?'

He didn't try to spare her feelings. 'Not that I know of. Why should she?'

Why, indeed? Because Natalie had known of her pregnancy, it didn't mean that her cousin had even considered the possibility of her being the girls' mother. Perdita hadn't told her she was expecting twins. 'In that case, I can just be their mother's distant cousin. At least they don't look like either of us.'

'Not too obviously, anyway. Just remember the document you signed this afternoon,' he said with harsh insistence.

She didn't need to be reminded. 'Oh, I do,' she said tonelessly.

'When are you going?'

'That's none of your business,' she returned, 'but don't worry, I'll keep in contact.'

She knew it sounded like a threat and she was pleased until she saw the expression on his face. Stark and potent, he looked at her with such a formidable impression of force and power that she was almost cowed.

For the first time she realised that her childhood impressions of Luke had not necessarily been correct. She had been infatuated with this man, made love with him, borne his children, and although he had cruelly driven her away she had understood his reaction—indeed, she had felt much the same as he had. But she had always thought of him as a gentleman.

Now, beneath the aristocratic bones and the polished veneer she recognised the authentic, chilling tang of the barbarian. Luke was fighting for his children, and if she met him head-on it would be a bloody, vicious, no-holds-barred battle.

He would use whatever means he needed to keep his daughters safe. If he thought she presented any danger to them at all, she'd find herself banished again. It seemed ridiculous to believe such a thing could happen in New Zealand, but she had no doubt that he'd find some way.

She said quietly, 'I want only what's best for the girls, Luke. I always have. If I hadn't, I'd have kept them, and they'd have grown up as I did, without stability. I knew I was too young. I learn from my experiences; I wasn't having my children go through that sort of childhood.' Looking away from him down the passage of the years, she said half to herself, 'Do you know that my father went back to his old life? Apparently, after a probationary period no one—least of all he and his wife—was in the least worried that he had seduced and abandoned my mother after making her pregnant. He kept his position, whereas my mother was subjected to the most appalling pressure to have me adopted, and when she wouldn't, was literally thrown out on to the street.'

Luke said relentlessly, 'Your mother was spoiled and headstrong and completely selfish. Think about it, Perdita. What sort of mother was she to you? The only reason she kept you was to make everyone suffer, you especially.'

He was cruelly perceptive, but what he didn't know was that her mother had truly loved Perdita's father; his defection had killed something in her. There had never been another man for Katherine Gladstone. Ill-equipped to earn her living, she had struggled for years, and because there hadn't been the support systems there were now for solo mothers she had been forced to leave her daughter with childminders while she worked at a succession of low-paying jobs. It didn't exactly make for good bonding.

Although not physically cruel, she had never made any attempt to love or understand the child she saw as the source of all her problems. Perdita had grown up knowing that her father had left her mother because she

had been conceived, that she was to blame for her
mother's unhappiness and their poverty.

Those bitter memories had led Perdita to give up her
twins.

'She suffered too,' she said now. 'Not that it matters—
it's all over and done with.' She hesitated, until some
dark compulsion made her ask, 'When you got my letter
did you believe it?'

His eyes were hooded. 'That you were their mother?
Yes, after I'd made enquiries.'

'And that they were yours?' For some reason she had
to know.

A muscle flicked in his jaw. 'Yes.' He paused, then
went on dispassionately, 'You'd been a virgin. They were
born eight and half months after that night. I knew they
had to be mine.'

What had he felt when he realised that the children
he'd adopted were his own daughters? One look at the
stark, impassive features revealed that she'd never know.

Besides, she wasn't sure she believed his version of
events. More than five years ago, well before she had
started seriously searching, someone had tried to make
sure that no one would ever be able to discover the twins'
identity. If it wasn't Luke, who had it been, and for what
reason?

She was never likely to know that, either, and now
was not the time to pursue it. So she nodded as though
the subject wasn't very interesting and said, 'I've done
what I wanted to. I've seen the twins and satisfied myself
that they're happy.' Casting a fleeting look at his implacable face, she touched her tongue to suddenly dry
lips and said more forcefully than she'd intended, 'I want
to keep in touch.'

'You are not to write——'

She said levelly, 'I want to keep in touch, Luke.' Resentment at his high-handedness broke through the guard
she'd set on her emotions. Without volition, her hand
stole up to touch the locket at her throat. 'I think you

owe me that, don't you? You've enjoyed them all their lives while I've spent untold hours wondering how they are, whether they've been loved as I'd have loved them, worrying that they might be mistreated, unhappy.'

He said harshly, 'You make it sound as though Natalie and I stole them. You gave them up.'

Her smile was the celebrated bittersweet one that had made her face hauntingly famous. 'It worked out very well for you, didn't it? I assume that it was Natalie who couldn't have children, but you got your own.'

'What the hell are you insinuating? That I deliberately set out to——?'

'Impregnate me, is that the term you're looking for?' Reining in her temper, she said more moderately, 'No, I know you didn't. I'm sorry, I'm behaving stupidly, but can't you see my point of view? Is it so strange that I want to keep in touch? You may not think I'm a very worthwhile character, but I swear to you that I would not willingly hurt them for anything in the world.'

'When you look at me like that I'd believe anything you say,' he said in a controlled voice that almost hid the hard-edged anger beneath the austere façade, 'and I have to remind myself that you've made a very good living these past years producing whatever looks you were asked for.'

Humiliation washed through her. Turning her head sharply so that he couldn't see what his brutal words had done to her, she fought it back. She wasn't ashamed of being a model. He was muddying the waters, diverting her attention from the point under discussion. She set her jaw. Excellent tactics, but they were going to fail because she had no intention of losing her children again. She didn't want to interfere in their lives—no, that was a lie.

Of course she wanted to be there for them, to see them all the time, but she accepted that it was impossible. When she had surrendered them for adoption she had given up her rights to mother them.

However, she hadn't given up her natural instincts, and she wanted to learn to understand her daughters, to be able to fathom the lights and shades of their personalities, to be someone to them. Losing Natalie must have wrenched them from happiness to insecurity, and Perdita wouldn't do anything to add to that. But she was going to be a part of their lives in some way.

She looked him square in the face and said collectedly, 'I mean it, Luke. Unless they ask me I won't tell them who I am, but sooner or later they'll want to know, and it would be easier for them if their birth mother is not a total stranger.'

'All right,' he said slowly. 'Give me your address.'

She could feel his reluctance, taste it on her tongue, and she knew how much effort it had cost him to say that. It was a major victory, but she was careful not to let him see her relief.

'I don't have one. I'll contact you when I get settled.'

They had been standing like antagonists, facing each other, eyes locked, searching for weaknesses, the air bristling with tension. Now Perdita felt awkward, the tension somehow metamorphosed into unease and embarrassment.

Her eyes slid away from the pale, cold intensity of his. 'Well,' she said awkwardly, 'thanks for coming to see whether I was all right. As you can see, I am.'

'You'd better wash the tearstains from your face,' he said curtly.

She put a hand to her cheek, felt the faint encrustations and pulled a face. 'Ugh.'

'Don't worry,' he said caustically, 'you could probably roll in mud and still come up looking like Helen of Troy and Eve mingled in one glorious woman. Tearstains merely add another dimension to that maddening smile. It's a wonder the advertising agency who dreamed up the Adventurous Woman project didn't think of them—they certainly thought of everything else.'

She said calmly, 'If they'd believed tears would sell more cosmetics they'd have done it. However, I was supposed to be an adventurous woman, not a wimp.'

'Why did you give modelling up? There isn't a flaw in that perfect face—I imagine you could have gone on for another five years yet. Ten, with filters.'

Perdita had spent years hearing her face and body discussed in the most clinical of terms, and would have said that she had no false vanity, no emotion but gratitude for the quirk of heredity that had given her looks and a body that matched the ideal for this decade. But something about the way Luke spoke sent a tiny whisper of foreboding through her.

He sounded every bit as blasé as her agent, as the photographers who'd called forth hundreds of incarnations of her. His gaze as it measured her high cheek-bones and satiny, full mouth was cool and dispassionate. Yet she detected an oblique anger, all the more intense for being so tightly leashed.

Many men had looked at her with desire. She was accustomed to it, knew how to deal with it. There was nothing in Luke's demeanour to indicate anything but a rigidly disciplined self-possession, but the air sparkled and quivered between them, and deep in her body a flicker of white-hot response flamed treacherously into life.

It had to be because she'd never had a chance to get over her crush on him. Most adolescents fell in and out of love until slowly they built up a pattern of under-standing, so that when real love arrived they recognised the differences. Pitchforked into an early maturity before she'd been ready to say goodbye to childhood, it was no wonder she was still in thrall to a purely physical response.

Caution steadied her voice, made her voice offhand as she shrugged. 'I'm not greedy. I've earned enough to make me secure for the rest of my life, and apart from interesting things like the Adventurous Woman pro-

motion, modelling was just sheer hard work after a
couple of years. I didn't enjoy being treated like a
commodity.'

Now why had she told him that? Her lashes covered
a momentarily uncertain gaze. Normally she wouldn't
have said that to anyone but a trusted friend. She didn't
trust Luke Dennison. She couldn't afford to. In many
ways he was the enemy, and, like all the most dangerous
ones, he had the ability to infiltrate her defences. Which
meant she was going to have to stop unbuttoning her lip
whenever he asked a simple question.

'Even though you conspired with a whole industry to
do exactly that? So we aren't going to see that lovely
face in any more magazines?'

'For a year or so,' she said, 'and then no.'

'What are you going to do?'

She shrugged again. 'I'll find something. I might go
to university.'

His hard mouth suddenly twisted into an enigmatic
smile. 'You'd cause a riot,' he said softly.

Perdita's breath caught in her throat. No, she thought.
No! She had to remember that this was just a hangover
from adolescence.

'As you see,' she said with unhurried self-possession,
'I don't look the way I do in the magazines.'

His brows lifted, but he said merely, 'Modest as well
as famous.'

A sudden weariness fogged her brain. She managed
to contrive a yawn and an enquiring look. He understood and his smile became even more sardonic. 'I'd
better go. Goodbye, Perdita.'

'Goodbye,' she said, trying to sound businesslike and
dismissive, but courteous nevertheless. An unnerving
glint in his eyes told her she hadn't succeeded.

She watched him go, her eyes unconsciously straying
to the breadth of his shoulders, the lean hips and taut
buttocks, the long, powerfully muscled legs. Closing the
door behind him with a sudden vicious jerk, she turned

and leaned back, her hands spread against the smooth, cool wood, her breath locked in her chest. She had lied when she said she didn't remember his lovemaking.

He had been tender, his hands slow and skilful as he caressed her into wakefulness. Bemused, her whole being singing with delight, she hadn't even thought of Natalie; she was lost to everything but the wonderful sensations that were rippling through her at the behest of those clever, experienced hands.

Darkness had hidden him, yet she hadn't been afraid. She'd known who he was. His scent, she thought now, trying to be objective. He had a particular male scent that still had the power to liquefy her bones. That night it had been spiked with the flavour of wine.

Her slow awakening had been something spun out of the fantasies she'd indulged in during the warm, welcoming nights of that summer. Still dreaming, her heart thudding like a piston in her chest, her mind drugged by the lazy tide of desire his touch summoned, she'd been gathered into his arms while his mouth searched for and finally, after a series of kisses, found the frantic pulse in her throat.

He hadn't spoken. If he had, she thought now, she'd probably have woken up to her danger, realised what was happening to her. She'd always loved him with the uncritical adoration of a child, but those holidays her serene, unashamed affection had altered into something deeper, forbidden. During the slow, heated days she had watched him, knowing that he never saw her, yet longing for him with a growing woman's intense passion, her ripening body aching with hidden, unfulfilled needs.

And each night just before she had dropped off to sleep she had called up images in her mind, telling herself guiltily that she was hurting nobody because nobody knew; nobody, especially Natalie, would ever know. Young and inexperienced though she was, she'd understood that such feverish emotions couldn't last, but when she'd woken in his arms she had had no defences from needs she had only just recognised.

His mouth seduced her into acquiesecence, his hands stroked a feverish response from her body; the fumes of her hunger hazed her brain to banish any moral restrictions she might have felt. Enslaved by the passion that shimmered through her like molten silver, the first love that until then had been so rigorously disciplined, she surrendered mindlessly.

His mouth on her breast set her shuddering, not with fear but with an awed delight at the exquisite pangs her body was capable of. She writhed voluptuously, seeking more, seeking something to ease the throbbing ache between her legs, pressing herself against the lean, heated body so close to hers. The unfamiliar pressure of his erection didn't shock her; instinct produced a swift, provoking answer from her hips, setting off chills through every nerve cell.

'Darling,' he'd said, 'such enthusiasm . . .'

Thinking about it made her heart weep. There had been such love, such lazy, amused tenderness in his tone.

Looking back with the awareness of experience she understood now that he had been immensely gentle, using his practised expertise to ready her until finally he had moved over her, and taken her in one slow, compulsive thrust, measuring the length of himself in her.

It hadn't hurt at all. Instead, everything within her had tightened in anticipation, sensations intensifying into a white-hot explosion, and she had gasped and opened herself to him, hips rotating, enclosing him with the force of her strong young body.

He had hesitated, his body rigid, but when she moved beneath him and around him he had groaned, and settled into a driving rhythm.

After that it had been all pleasure, keen, sharp delight edged with the promise of rapture.

The rapture hadn't come. She had been striving for it, her head tossed back on the pillows, little moans forcing their way through her lips, when suddenly Luke had cried out and his massive body had driven even deeper. As he had shaken in the throes of his climax she had realised—too late, God help her—what she'd allowed to happen.

In that bitter moment, the moment the twins were conceived, she had been scourged by the enormity of her behaviour. She had betrayed her best friend and mentor, the woman who had taken her in hand and taught her all that she knew, the cousin to whom she owed everything. Even the nightgown Luke had taken off had been bought for her by Natalie in that small orgy of clothes-buying they had indulged in before she'd come up to Pigeon Hill.

Stabbed by the sudden impact of her own treachery, she had moaned and tried desperately to free herself from his weight. The unfulfilled ripples of rapture ebbed and died, to be replaced by horror and a corrosive sense of defilement that had never really left her.

It had been reinforced by his reaction when the rigors of ecstasy had left him.

Even now, almost eleven years later, she could recall everything with an exactness that still made her feel sick. Listening to the sound of his car dying away in the quiet air, she turned the light off and opened a curtain, staring out into the darkness. She had forced the memories down, done her best to forget them, but in vain; newly minted and fresh, sound, sight, scent, the taste of him in her mouth, the exquisite tactile sensation of his skin against hers, they lurked unchanged.

'Natalie?' he said, and she shrivelled at the note of hope in his voice.

'No, no, it's not,' she gabbled, the words falling like hideous oaths into air scented with their lovemaking.

The change in him, the shock and then the anger, were like blows on an already smarting body. With the deadly intentness of a hunting animal he left her, rolling over in the bed to switch on the light. Perdita covered her face with her hands, swift tears scorching her eyes, eyes that were still dilated with the frustrated promise of fulfilment.

'What the hell are you doing here?' he demanded in a voice raw with fury. 'Where's Natalie?'

She tried to explain, but she choked with fear and a terrified recognition that something had happened which would affect all of their lives forever.

'*Where is she?*'

'She's at the Gardiners'—in Wellsford—she said——'

The words fell unheeded into silence.

'So you decided it was the perfect opportunity to satisfy the itch you've had all summer. You sneaking, conniving little bitch,' he said slowly, such promise of retribution in his voice that she truly feared for her life. His hand dragged hers away from her eyes. Childishly, she kept her wet eyelids pressed shut until he said in a voice that brooked no disobedience, 'Look at me.'

Her lashes fluttered up. He looked at her with hatred, unsparing contempt icing the fury in his expression. Perdita saw hell in a man's eyes, a glacial detachment that swallowed the last heat of slaked desire as though it had never existed.

'You're just like your mother,' he said distinctly. 'Didn't her experience teach you anything? Get out of my bed—and out of my life. I don't ever want to see you again, do you hear?'

Like a man imprisoned in a fortress of bitter darkness, an armour of bleak savagery clamping down around him, he stared at her as though she had killed something rare and precious to him, something he would never regain.

'Yes,' Perdita whispered. It was all she could say, and even then she had to propel the word past a dry, painful throat.

'Tomorrow you'll go back to Auckland. If Natalie——' he swallowed, before continuing harshly '—if she gets back before you leave Pigeon Hill you'll tell her that your mother rang. She's found you a holiday job. And you'll take every last thing that is yours from this house and never come back. Do you hear me?'

Mesmerised by the frozen fire licking at the back of his eyes, her body taut with pain and rejection, Perdita nodded.

'And if you tell Natalie about this,' he said in a level, implacable tone, 'I'll make your life so wretched you'll wish you'd died before you ever came up with the idea.'

She whispered, 'Luke, I didn't, I swear——'

'I don't want to listen to your lies,' he snarled, rising from the bed. 'Get out, Perdita. Just go, before I forget I'm supposed to be a civilised man and do what I want to do to you: make you pay in full for this.'

In deep shock, she clutched the pretty nightgown to her chest and raced back to her own bed.

By dawn she had everything packed. She couldn't go down to breakfast. The thought of food made her feel ill, but it was the prospect of meeting Luke—or even worse, Natalie—that kept her hiding in her bedroom. Shortly after nine someone tapped on the door. Natalie, she thought with a sickening shudder, sure that her guilt was written on her face.

But Luke stood there. Perdita kept her eyes lowered as he said with frigid antagonism, 'Natalie's not back yet. I'll drive you in.'

She nodded. On the way into Manley he said, 'If anything happens, you must tell me straight away.'

Had he been thinking even then that if their coupling proved fertile he would take her children? In the lonely motel room Perdita shivered. She would never know, because Luke certainly wasn't going to tell her.

She had said, 'Yes, all right,' unable to keep the tears from strangling her voice.

'Stop that.' That cold loathing in his voice had compounded her despair.

Too overwrought to dissemble, she whispered, 'I really didn't know, Luke—ask Natalie.'

He didn't believe her. But when Natalie came back she'd make that right—at least then he'd know that Perdita hadn't deliberately seduced him. During the long reaches of the night she had accepted that she could never go back to Pigeon Hill but at least it was some small compensation that he would know she had been innocent of the horrible accusations he'd made.

'Remember what I said—Natalie must never know.'

The lethal menace in his voice chilled her to the centre of her soul. 'No, oh, no!'

The sheer horror in her tone must have convinced him. He said with a curt, relentless anger that made her quail, 'Don't come back again.'

'No.'

It was a death knell. She felt so unworthy, so wicked, so sordid.

Looking back now, she could weep for the child she had been. She had told her irritated mother that Natalie and Luke were entertaining, and Katherine had accepted that in that case, of course they wouldn't want her there.

Months later, when she had to admit pregnancy, she had had her position in Katherine's life underlined yet again.

'You stupid little *idiot*!' her mother said scathingly. 'Well, I'm not going to put up with morning sickness and seeing you sit around getting more and more gross by the day. You'll have to go into a home.'

A week later Perdita had been deposited like a sack of unwanted goods in a nursing home. Katherine hadn't even asked who the father was.

They had been kind to her in the home, and she had quite enjoyed being there. With hindsight, she could see that she had been caught in shock so deep that it induced a paralysed detachment. It had never occurred to her to tell Luke; she blocked him from her mind.

And then one day Natalie had arrived. 'I have my methods,' she had laughed when a stunned and dismayed Perdita had asked how she knew.

She hadn't condemned at all; she'd been bright and affectionate and funny, but guilt had kept Perdita almost silent and wary. Natalie hadn't seemed to mind. Although Perdita watched her fearfully it was obvious that she had no idea that Luke had fathered Perdita's children. In fact, they hadn't talked about them at all.

There had been one sticky moment.

As Natalie was leaving, Perdita had asked, 'You won't tell anyone, will you?'

Natalie's brows lifted. 'No, I won't.'

'Not even Luke.' Her tongue was swollen and clumsy when she said his name; she had to force it out.

Natalie gave her a hug. 'I don't tell Luke everything,' she said, and Perdita had been satisfied. It was something she could do for both Natalie and Luke; if either knew he was the father it would make unbearable complications. She knew Luke well enough to understand that he would feel responsible for the children, and for her. If he found out, Natalie might too, and Perdita couldn't have borne that.

Natalie hadn't come back, and Perdita had been glad. She didn't want to see anyone who reminded her of those impassioned moments in Luke's arms. In the cloistered surroundings of the nursing home she was almost able to forget what had led to her stay there.

And now, she thought, staring out into the darkness of a northern New Zealand winter's night, what am I going to do now?

This was how she had felt after she had left her daughters in the nursing home. Rootless, abandoned, so deeply depressed that she was exhausted all the time. Finishing school was unthinkable; a gulf separated her from other people of her own age.

Miraculously, she'd found the job in a model agency office. When they wanted a reference she had summoned the courage to visit Clive, Natalie's designer, and ask him for one. Solely because she was Natalie's cousin he'd rung the agency manager and whatever he'd said had done the trick.

Only a week after she'd got the job, while she was still trying to fathom out how to work the computer, she'd been dragged into a television ad when one of the proper models failed to turn up. The camera had signified its undying devotion, and from then on her career had been meteoric. A trip to model in Japan had been followed by one to Milan, and then she'd been taken up by one of the topmost agencies in New York and never looked back.

It wasn't, she thought cynically, going to be quite so easy this time. Before she had seen her children she thought that was all she wanted to do, simply reassure herself of their welfare and happiness.

Now she was greedy. She wanted so much more.

And Luke was standing in her way.

CHAPTER THREE

THE motel bed was too short, but that wasn't the reason Perdita didn't sleep well that night. Scraps of the conversation with her daughters kept floating into her consciousness, exciting her anew, yet her dreams were dark and disturbed by images from the past. Finally, she gave up trying to sleep and lay sorting through her thoughts, trying to bring some sort of order to them.

She recalled her cousin's magnetism, her enthusiasm and the patience with which she'd taken a shy, socially retarded girl and managed to coax her out of her shell and into the light of the real world. After a while it no longer mattered to Perdita that her mother didn't love her, because Natalie had love to spare. She owed her cousin far more than the small amount of charm she possessed. Sometimes she thought she owed Natalie her ability to love.

And Natalie had loved her children.

Although she'd known it wasn't going to be easy, she hadn't realised that coming back to Manley was going to be quite so complicated. Nevertheless, she thought as she stretched restlessly, it was worth it. Seeing Rosalind and Olivia had eased the piercing sense of displacement that had been her constant companion all her life. Whatever happened, however this turned out, she knew she had some foothold in the future.

Just after eight the next morning the telephone's shrill summons interrupted her solitary breakfast. Putting down her spoon, Perdita looked at the receiver with a caution she knew to be foolish.

After a moment she reached out and picked it up. 'Yes?'

'Perdita?'

The voice raised tendrils of memory. 'Yes,' she repeated carefully.

'Perdita, it's Juliette. I used to be Juliette Joseph, but I'm Juliette Robinson now.'

Memory clicked into place. Juliette Joseph's father had owned a fishing lodge on the shores of the Whangaroa Harbour; although older than Luke and Natalie, he and his wife had often visited Pigeon Hill with their daughter, a bright, mischievous girl a couple of years younger than Perdita.

'Hello,' Perdita said. 'Don't tell me you actually managed to marry Peter!'

Juliette gave a startled gurgle of laughter. 'Yep, five years ago. He fought a good fight to the bitter end, but the stronger woman won. We live in Paihia now, and we're running a diving school and shop in the Bay.'

'It's great to hear from you. How did you know I was here?'

'Oh, you know the Bay! As soon as you set foot inside the place everyone knows your business and who you slept with the night before. Maura Seagrave saw you walking down the street in Manley and recognised you, so she rang me with the news. I rang Pigeon Hill, and Luke told me you were here' She laughed. 'I dithered a bit about actually contacting you, because I thought you might have gone all worldly and snooty on us, but Luke said you'd probably like to hear from me.'

'He was correct. I'm not in the least worldly or snooty!'

'I didn't really think you would be. Listen, I've got to get off to the shop, but would you like to come to dinner tonight? I'd love to catch up with you—and I'm so impressed. You're the only famous person I know, except for Fraser Thornquist, and you're much prettier than he is, although he wouldn't believe that. You're nicer, too.'

'I should hope so!'

'Do you know him?'

Perdita pulled a face. 'Very slightly.' The star of a
popular television cop show had made a nuisance of
himself one year at the Paris prêt-à-porter shows, refusing to believe that Perdita simply wasn't interested in
his flashy, already raffish charms.

'Wow, you really have been moving in high circles!
Do you like him?'

'No.'

Juliette laughed. 'Neither did I. Octopus hands. Pete
had to threaten to throw him off the boat before he
finally accepted that I wasn't on the menu. Can you come
to dinner, Perdita?'

For the first time in years there was no programme
mapped out for Perdita, no appointments she had to
keep. For years she had longed for the time when her
life was her own, so it was ironic that it seemed to stretch
out in front of her like an endless riverbed choked with
sand—flat, featureless and barren.

'I'd love to,' she said, and jotted down the directions
to Juliette's house, thinking that it just went to show
that it was the journey, not the destination, that was
important.

She finished her cereal, and drank orange juice that
tasted fresher than any other in the world, probably because the fruit had been picked from the big Washington
navel tree she could see through her window and
squeezed by hand only half an hour before. The sun
poured through the window on to the small table, high-
lighting with a cruelly exact eye the brown carpet and
sunflower-splashed duvet on the bed, both showing signs
of hard wear.

It was a far cry from luxury hotels and the modern
airiness of her loft apartment in New York, but she didn't
miss either the luxury or the space. Last night she had
slept with her window open—held by security catches,
admittedly—and the fresh, sweet air had poured in,
scented with starlight and dew and the soft exhalations
of grass and plants.

Smiling, she picked up the paperback she had bought in an Auckland bookshop. *Gardens to Visit*, the cover said, and there were three within a twenty-mile radius. She had planned to see one on the way back; now, with a whole day to spend, she could visit all three of them. And not too far away was an art gallery in a magnificent house set in yet another recommended garden. Yes, she'd enjoy her day.

That night, knowing that it would be casual, she dressed carefully for the dinner. A pair of sand-coloured trousers in linen, with a silk blouse in sand and olive stripes and a slightly darker sand cashmere jersey, was redeemed from complete informality by excellent cut and understated, luxurious fabrics. Slipping on a canary diamond ring, she admired its glowing golden heart for a moment, then set out towards Paihia and a pleasant evening.

The first person she saw as she walked in through the door of Juliette's pleasant house, high on the hill over-looking the magnificent panorama of the Bay of Islands, was Luke, big and saturnine and aloof in what was clearly the guest of honour's chair. He had, her hostess told her, been in Whangarei all day, which was why Juliette hadn't asked him to bring Perdita.

He knew she was coming; there was no surprise in the pale eyes as he got to his feet. Wishing that Juliette had told her there were to be other guests, Perdita smiled warily.

'Hello, Perdita,' he said.

There was no condemnation in his voice, but she read it in his level, unsettling look, and shot him a sparkling glance in return. This was none of her organising!

Fortunately Juliette had decided that four people were enough for her dinner. Or perhaps it was unfortunate. Perdita had never felt less like talking to people she barely knew, but the very intimacy of the occasion meant she couldn't relax.

It wasn't too difficult for the first part of the evening. Juliette and her husband, a man of medium height with the lean, blocky build of a diver and a receding hairline above a pleasant, shrewd face, were content to play 'do you remember', and Perdita found it easy to join them.

But inevitably, over an excellent meal, that subject died, and they began to talk of other things. Juliette was fascinated by Perdita's high-flying career, so like a conjuror Perdita produced more incidents, mostly amusing, all slightly outrageous and entertaining, a little more racy than the ones she'd entertained the twins with the day before.

She kept both her hosts laughing and intrigued, but a swift survey from beneath her lashes at the other member of the quartet revealed that he wasn't fooled. The slight smile that curved his mouth had undertones of irony to it, and there was cynical comprehension in his eyes. He knew perfectly well what she was doing— deflecting any deeper enquiries with superficial anecdotes.

'Oh, it sounds so glamorous,' Juliette sighed. 'I used to look at your picture in the magazines and wonder how on earth lanky Perdita Gladstone had turned into this haughty, elegant creature. I can see how, now. You always had the bones.'

'Sheer good fortune,' Perdita said briskly. 'There are swarms of much better-looking women out there, but because I'm tall and skinny clothes drape wonderfully on me, and the camera for some strange reason adores my face. I was lucky.'

'Ah, but you move so gracefully. I used to envy you so much; even when you were a kid you moved with such natural, inborn grace it was like watching— oh——' Lost for words, Juliette looked appealingly around the table.

'According to Natalie, something strange and wondrous from the depths of time,' Luke supplied.

Juliette nodded. 'Yes, that's it. But what's this about the camera loving your face? Such modesty! You're stunning to look at, you must know that.'

'I know how to dress,' Perdita said lightly. 'That's easily learned. And I know how to use cosmetics, and a thousand different ways of doing my hair. And don't forget that those finished photographs that appear in the magazines are not really me; they were all taken after hours spent being made up and having my hair done and being dressed. Even then the photographer uses every trick of the trade to get the effect the advertiser or magazine wants. And that's not all; there's always the airbrush hovering in the wings.'

'Does it worry you,' Luke asked with a cool, un-smiling glance, 'that you are an impossible ideal?'

A shadow passed over Perdita's face. 'Yes,' she acknowledged reluctantly. 'At first it never occurred to me, but lately I've realised just how much harm that sort of idealisation can do.'

Juliette said indignantly, 'What on earth are you talking about? Everyone knows that those photos are dressed to within an inch of their lives—no one sensible takes them seriously.'

'Don't let anyone in the fashion business hear you say that!' But Perdita's smile soon faded. 'Are you on a diet, Juliette?'

Her hostess looked astonished, then a little guiltily down at her plate. 'Well—I am trying to lose weight,' she admitted.

Perdita said, 'Yet medical opinion is swinging around to the view that dieting only makes you fat. Once you get on that treadmill you're in trouble. And the sad thing is that you're not overweight. Oh, you're not so thin you could pass through the eye of a needle, but then only a few genetic freaks are that.'

'Exactly what I tell her,' Peter concurred eagerly. 'I like her the way she is. This dieting is just plain ridiculous.'

'That's easy for you to say,' Juliette flared. 'You dive all your weight off, but if I don't diet I'll just get bigger and bigger.' She flashed a resentful glance at Perdita. 'I suppose you can eat like a horse and never put weight on.'

'As I said, a genetic freak.'

Luke asked, 'Was your newfound conviction that this is bad for the rest of womanhood the reason you gave it up?' The note of irony in his voice intensified, as did the insolent appraisal in his eyes.

'Partly,' Perdita said. 'The other part is that as well as being damned hard work it's mind-bogglingly dull. That famous sulky, haughty look is usually the result of extreme boredom. I'm not knocking it; it's been good to me, and most of the people I met love their jobs and would be horrified to be accused of exploiting women's gullibility.'

'And, of course, it's extremely profitable,' Luke said gently. 'For everyone. It sounds almost as though you're biting the hand that fed you very well.'

She subdued her anger with an effort of will. 'Perhaps. It has its good points, too. It's one of the few jobs where a woman's looks *don't* work against her. Of course, it means that nobody ever takes you seriously again, but hey, you can't have everything, and there are plenty of women out in the world who don't get taken seriously because of their looks, whether good or bad.'

There was a sharp little silence, a silence Juliette hurried to fill. 'Well, it's certainly a different outlook on a world I'd rather taken for granted. I see you're wearing your trademark locket.' She laughed teasingly and widened her eyes. 'Whose photo do you have in it?'

Perdita's hand came up to cover the thin oval of warm gold. 'Oh, no one's,' she said vaguely.

'It's just a gimmick, then?'

Damn, but she was persistent. Perdita's smile didn't waver. 'My agent was rather good at that sort of thing,' she said smoothly, removing her hand. 'It became my trademark, helped get me recognised, gave journalists a handle when they wrote about me.'

'Clever,' Luke said thoughtfully, his eyes on the small ornament around her slender throat.

Perdita moved slightly, and the locket slid down beneath the silk of her shirt.

'Very clever,' Juliette agreed. 'That's what we need, Peter, an inspired idea for publicity purposes. Ah well, perhaps we'll come up with one some day. What are you planning to do, Perdita, now that you've retired?'

'I'm not sure,' Perdita said. She smiled around the table, carefully not catching anyone's eye. 'I'll find something. Now tell me about this venture of yours. It sounds fascinating. Didn't I hear you say something about abseiling? I'd quite like to have a go at that.'

Juliette and Peter were only too eager to talk about their fledgling business, and the rest of the dinner passed with an abundance of good talk and laughter. Perdita was surprised to find herself with a second glass of wine in her hand. Normally abstemious, she couldn't remember the first one going down. Oddly unnerved, she set the glass aside.

It was late when at last they went outside. Shivering in the sudden chill, Perdita stood for a moment to look down at the lights of Paihia. The pale sliver of a vagrant moon had just winked out from behind a cloud, limning it with silver. Calm and still, with a deep, barely perceptible sheen beneath the star-embossed sky, the sea lay like a silken blanket between the dark, rough headlands. The air was cold and crisp and fresh, tanged with the scent of salt.

Behind her, Juliette and Peter were standing in the doorway, arms around each other's waists, laughing, waving goodbye.

Perdita was assailed by a sense of loss, of disconnection. She had never known a home; the succession of flats she had lived in with her mother had been stark

shells devoid of warmth or comfort because Katherine's
bitterness had leached away any regard or affection.

And in spite of her love for it, Pigeon Hill had never
been home, either.

Juliette and Peter saw in her a creature from another
world, flashing through theirs for a short while before
orbiting out again. They didn't realise how lucky they
were.

Even her children, carried under her heart for the best
part of a year, were not hers; brought up by others, their
characters had been moulded, their opinions formed by
Natalie and Luke.

Oh, why don't you *wallow* in self-pity while you're
about it? she thought sturdily, turning to wave once more
at her hostess. You have more than most women of your
age; all you need is a worthwhile job. Eventually you'll
find someone and you'll know him when you see him.
He'll be love and peace and rest for you, your anchor
to the world.

And while common sense told her that no man could
be all that, she still hoped for a miracle.

'I'll follow you home,' Luke said as he opened her
car door for her.

Nodding, she murmured, 'Thank you.'

She could have protested, but it wouldn't have made
any difference. In Luke's world women were the weaker
sex, to be watched over when it came to things like
driving along a darkened road late at night.

They had been travelling for ten minutes and were
through Paihia when a car came roaring up behind Luke,
shot past him and into the gap between them, and then
with a multitude of beeps from the horn and the sound
of fists banging on doors tore past Perdita on the outside
of a corner.

'Hoons,' she thought angrily, her foot stabbing the
brake. Automatically her eyes flicked to the rear vision
mirror. Luke had dropped back but he was coming nearer
again now.

Perhaps it was that quick glance, or perhaps because she wasn't yet accustomed to driving on the left, but when she rounded the next corner she didn't see the car on the side of the road until almost too late. This time her foot stamped on the brake; the tyres responded with a screech as they bit into the tarseal, then the car skidded in the heavy dew across the road and into the ditch.

The seatbelt saved her from any serious injury, but something hit her knee and pain shot up her arm. She gave a grunting, gasping cry and slumped down, fighting for control.

By the time she had emerged from the self-absorption engendered by pain and shock she could hear nothing but Luke's urgent voice. 'Are you all right?' he was demanding as he wrenched the door open. 'Perdita, are you all right?'

His touch on her arm made her yelp. 'Sorry,' he said, removing it smartly. His voice sharpened. 'Where is it? Where are you hurt?'

'My wrist,' she muttered, cradling it. 'It feels as though it's broken.'

'Hold it steady. Anything else?' he asked, running a hand down her body. 'How are your legs?'

'My knee's a bit painful, but I can move my leg. I'm all right, except for my wrist.' She tried to move it, stopping immediately as sweat popped out in beads on her forehead. 'Damn, that hurts,' she said through tight lips. 'Are you all right?'

'Yes. I saw them just in time. They took off when you went into the ditch.' The beam of a torch strayed over her face, making her blink. 'No, it doesn't look as though you've got concussion,' he said, ignoring her irritable complaint. The light left her face and flashed downwards. 'No blood,' he said. 'Wriggle your toes.'

They moved freely and without pain in her shoes.

'All right. Does it hurt to breathe?'

'A little,' she said, 'but that's only bruising from the seatbelt. I know what a cracked rib feels like, and nothing's damaged there.'

'Good. Head aching?'

'Slightly.'

'Look at me.'

Gingerly she turned towards him, and was rewarded by a softening in his voice. 'Any pain?'

'Only a bit.'

'It looks as though you've got off comparatively lightly.' He leaned in and wrapped a rug around her, saying, 'I've called for help on the carphone. I'm going to have to leave you for a moment because I can hear something coming, and I want to flag them down. All right?'

'Yes, of course.'

But she missed his steady, reassuring presence. Until the ambulance came she huddled against the seat and tried to fight off her reaction with willpower.

Two hours later, bandaged, with a packet of pills for the pain tucked into her bag, she was in Luke's big Mercedes, aching as though she had been put through a particularly merciless wringer. At the hospital some twenty miles from Manley they'd X-rayed her and prodded her until they'd finally agreed that the worst damage was a badly sprained wrist.

'What's going to happen to the car?' she asked, looking out at the barely darker outlines of the hills. No lights gleamed in the farmhouses along the way, no cars came towards them or overtook them. It was like being at the end of time.

'I've made all the arrangements. The towtruck's already collected it and taken it to a garage in Paihia. Who have you insured it with?'

She told him and he said, 'I'll contact them to-morrow. Don't worry about it.'

It was probably bad for her, but just this once she was going to let him take over.

They were almost at Pigeon Hill when she roused herself enough to realise where she was. Then she blurted, 'I can't stay here.'

'I'm afraid you'll have to.' He made no attempt to pretend that he wanted her there. In a voice completely lacking in expression he went on, 'You heard the doctor say that it'll be a couple of days before you can look after yourself. Don't fuss, Perdita. This is what you wanted, isn't it? A chance to get to know the girls better?'

Yes, of course it was, but not here, she thought in confusion, her normal composure shattered. This was Natalie's home, impressed with Natalie's personality. Guilt and grief were powerful bedfellows.

'I can't put you to all this trouble,' she said with a show of spirit. 'I'll hire a nurse.'

'Don't be silly. And it won't be me you're putting to trouble, it will be Barbara.'

'Is she still here?'

'Yes. She's staying at the homestead tonight as it happens; she's been very good helping out with the girls.'

Perdita nodded, her eyelids drooping. A yawn worked its way through her. Utterly exhausted, she leaned her head back on the seat as they rattled across the cattlestop.

'Besides,' he said aloofly, 'you're in shock.'

She was certainly in something. When she scrambled out of the car her legs wouldn't hold her. She muttered a sharp, almost voiceless curse, but he noticed. A powerful arm caught her around the shoulders, holding her upright.

'Shall I carry you in?' he asked unhurriedly.

'No,' she sighed. 'I'm not sick, or faint. Just shaky.'

'As I said, shock.'

He supported her up the steps and into the house. Inside it was warm and smelled of a faint mixture of flowers and beeswax and something else she could never remember smelling in any other house; the scent of a happy home, she'd always thought. Once her main ambition had been to have a house that smelled like that.

Now she didn't have any ambitions; she couldn't see herself with a husband and more children. All her emotional investment seemed tied up here at Pigeon Hill.

He took her to the room she used to sleep in, a small narrow bedroom with a view out over the dark bulk of Pukekukupa. Nothing seemed to have changed in either of the other two rooms she'd seen, but this was quite different from the way it used to be. The white coverlet had given place to one of blue and gold stripes, and lacquered pieces replaced the softly blonded furniture. Instead of the charming Victorian prints on the walls there were water-colours of the local scenery.

'I'll send Barbara in to help you undress,' Luke said from the doorway.

'No, I'll manage. One thing being a model teaches you is the ability to cope with dressing in peculiar situations. I've wriggled out of far more complicated outfits than this in far less room, with someone applying make-up and someone else doing my hair.' She was gabbling, her runaway tongue refusing to be silenced until she used all her willpower to rein it in.

His eyes gleamed suddenly, but he said nothing more than, 'Goodnight, then. I probably won't see you in the morning; I have to be in Kaitaia for a meeting. Sleep well.'

An exhausting fifteen minutes later she was resigned to sleeping in her bra, silk pants and the locket and chain. Her clothes seemed possessed of devils, and while struggling to get out of them she'd managed to give her wrist a couple of good knocks that left her white with pain and temper.

Now she was going to have to wash her face. She was sitting on the edge of the bed working up the strength to walk along to the bathroom when someone tapped on the door.

She shot to her feet. 'Wait a minute!' The thready note of hysteria in her voice disgusted her as much as her self-pity had before.

There was nothing to hide behind. She gave the bed-cover a panicked tug, but it resisted, and if he should decide to open the door she'd be almost completely exposed to his cold gaze. Her bra was nothing more than a wisp of net, completely transparent, and the knickers didn't hide much more.

Snatching up her silk shirt, she held it in front of herself like a shield and approached the door, intending to open it only a crack. The handle resisted her fumbling attempts—the first thing I'm going to do in my retirement is learn to be ambidextrous, she vowed grimly—and to her horror she felt it turn smoothly from the other side.

The heavy wooden door hit her bare foot. Smothering a yelp of pain, she jerked backwards, hit her sore knee on the wooden frame of a chair and collapsed on to the bed.

'What the hell——?' Luke pushed the door fully open, his lean, dark face set in lines of exasperated concern.

'It's nothing—I just had my foot in the way, it's all right,' she babbled, huddling behind the totally inadequate shield of her shirt.

His face hardened. After one comprehensive glance he looked resolutely down at her feet. Perdita's skin prickled over bones unexpectedly rendered useless.

Uncertainly, she said, 'I'm all right, thank you.'

He had a towel in his hand, and what appeared to be a nightgown and robe over his arm. Dropping them on to the bed, he knelt in front of her, his hand going out to pick up her foot.

'It's bruising already,' he said in an odd, raw voice.

His touch was warm and incredibly gentle. Heat crawled up from Perdita's chest; gripping the shirt in one hand, she stealthily picked up the towel and draped it across her body and thighs.

'It's not hurting,' she lied, looking down at his bent head. In defiance of its strictly conventional cut, the auburn-tinged hair curled at the nape of his neck.

Something sweet and forbidden tugged fiercely deep inside her as his fingers moved carefully over the fragile contours of her foot, coming to rest at the place where the door had opened on it.

'I bruise easily,' she said desperately, wondering how the sight of those curls, and his tanned hands against the Celtic pallor of her skin, could scramble every thought in her brain.

The lights danced dizzily in his hair as he looked up. 'I'll get some ice,' he said.

'No, it's all right. Don't fuss, Luke.'

She hated being so shaky and exposed, hated being reduced to feebly shrinking back on the bed with a towel held around her. Luke's presence filled the room, over-powering her with fierce male dominance. Sharp little stabs of excitement chased through her.

'What are you afraid of?' he asked remotely, getting to his feet.

Her gaze travelled up, skidded past the telltale hardness that told her he too was aroused. She flinched at the glittering aura of sexuality around him.

She whispered, 'Go away, please, Luke.'

'Why did you come here, Perdita?' he asked, his voice reflective, almost emotionless.

'You know why. To see my children,' she said angrily.

She made the mistake of looking up into his face, and saw with a quiver of her heart that his intent eyes were tracing the soft line of her lips, the long, slender arc of her throat, the sweep of milk-white, translucent skin across her shoulders, the way the thin gold chain that supported her locket fell into the hollow of her throat.

'Did you think there might be a place here for you now that Natalie's dead?' he asked, his even voice reinforcing the insulting, relentless scrutiny. 'I suppose it must have seemed the perfect solution. After all, you're getting a little old for displaying yourself in front of cameras. And presumably none of the men with whom you've enjoyed such public——' he invested the word with patrician disgust '—liaisons came up to scratch and offered you marriage. Now that you've had your fun you want to settle down. And who better than with the man who took your virginity and gave you children, the man who has your children?'

'Get out of here!' Scarlet with outrage and a queer shame, she was furious with him and with herself, because there might have been the slightest tang of truth to his words. Although Natalie's death had devastated her, had she wondered—not consciously, but in some obscure, proscribed corner of her mind—whether she could take her cousin's place in the children's lives?

His forefinger came out and flicked the locket out from the shroud of the towel, holding it in the palm of his hand. Beneath his touch Perdita's skin flamed. Breath blocked in her throat, her startled gaze was held prisoner by the sheer, mesmerising force of his.

'Whose portrait is in the locket?' he asked.

Shivering, aware that he'd attribute the colour that so blatantly flooded her skin to guilt, she jerked the locket free from his grasp and clenched her hand around it, glaring up into his harshly contoured face, her eyes spitting green sparks.

'Nobody you know,' she said, the words snapping like cracks of a whip. 'Get out of here, Luke.'

There was a heart-shaking moment, then, 'Gladly,' he bit out, turning towards the door with something less than his usual smooth masculine grace.

When the door closed behind him Perdita shivered, her swift colour dying, taking the warmth with it.

The nightgown was a T-shirt, never worn and big enough to slip easily over her shoulders without too much in the way of contortions. Perdita looked down at the dark blue material, and suddenly the hot, unbidden tears came. With a trembling hand she got into it and pulled the wrap on, waiting until the stifled sobs died before she walked to the bathroom along the hall.

When she got back to her room there was a plastic bag full of ice in a bowl on the bedside table. Refusing to give way to the weariness that seemed to come from her bones, she folded the ice pack around her foot.

Luke was right: it did help. Half an hour later she put the bag of melting cubes into the bowl and crawled into bed, exhausted, shaking with the knowledge that she was still violently, elementally attracted to him.

And that he wanted her as well as despised her. Oh, he had tried to hide it, using his vicious tongue to lash at her, but the body had signals, secret and not so secret, that made a liar of the mind and the will.

What kept her awake, however, was the shameful pleasure she found in this. Somehow, in spite of the fact that she knew how easy it was for a man to desire a woman, his undeclared hunger had soothed some raw place in her soul. She had never realised before just how much it had hurt that the tenderness, the heartshaking desire, the heat of his kisses, the feverish, passionate consummation, had all been Natalie's.

Now she had something of her own.

Despise herself as she did for that feeling, it wouldn't go away.

Perhaps, she thought as she slowly drifted off to sleep, that was why she hadn't been able to fall in love. Oh, she had tried. Two years after she left New Zealand she had met a man she respected, and almost fallen in love with him. Funny and kind and intelligent, he was generally considered to be sexy, but each of the several times they made love she had felt nothing beyond a mild pleasure.

It hadn't been fair to him, so she had said goodbye, breaking his heart in the process. The experience had been shattering, one she had never been tempted to repeat. The other men she had been seen with had known she wasn't going to sleep with them, but as they had wanted her company for other reasons than the sexual, they had been content with her presence on their arms.

Apparently to be seen with one of the world's most highly paid models gave a distinct fillip to masculine prestige. Only she and the men concerned knew the truth, and she wasn't going to tell anyone.

Not even Luke, who could think what he liked.

CHAPTER FOUR

NEXT morning she was woken by a tap on the door and the arrival of a woman bearing a tray. Dazed by late, heavy sleep, Perdita stared at her in consternation, wondering for one awful moment where she was.

'Hello, Perdita; remember me?' the woman said, accurately guessing her state of mind. 'Barbara Whittaker? You had an accident on the way home last night and Luke brought you here.'

Perdita sat up, wincing as she pushed hair back from her face with the hand attached to her sprained wrist. 'Of course I remember you,' she said through clenched teeth that held back a yawn. 'It's lovely to see you again. How are you? And how's Bob?'

The tray was deposited on the bedside table. Efficiently, Barbara Whittaker plumped pillows and dropped them behind Perdita's back before transferring the tray to her lap. 'We're both fine, thank you. No need to ask how you are—you look wonderful. Now, Luke tells me you've been in the wars. How's the wrist this morning?'

Wriggling it experimentally, Perdita pulled a face. 'Sore.'

'I thought toast would probably be the easiest to eat. Is that all right?'

'It looks delicious, but you shouldn't be waiting on me.'

'Luke said you needed your sleep. I'll butter that for you, shall I, and put the marmalade on? The girls wanted to come in, but I managed to convince them you'd still be here when they came home from school, so they had a wonderful time tiptoeing around like conspirators.

They like a bit of drama. Luke's on his way to Kaitaia. He said to have a quiet day, and rest that wrist.'

'I'm not going to do much else,' Perdita said.

'I'll be up in an hour to help you dress,' the housekeeper said. Perdita's face must have been eloquent because the older woman gave her sympathetic smile. 'No, you don't have to get into the same clothes. Luke went into the motel and picked up all your gear before he left.'

'How kind of him.' Perdita's voice was carefully bland.

Barbara looked surprised. 'Yes, it was, but that's Luke. No matter how busy he is, he'll help a friend. Mind you, he's had to give up a lot of his outside interests since Natalie died.'

'How have you all managed?'

Barbara pushed the curtains back. 'At first it was really hard. The girls wandered around like little lost souls, and I seemed to spend most of my time comforting them instead of doing the housework, but they're over the worst now, and we've organised a roster system that's working reasonably well.' She twitched an ornament on the dressing-table into place. 'Luke's been marvellous with them. We all do our best, but it's not the same as Mother for them.'

'One of these days,' Perdita said unevenly, 'I'd like to talk to you about Natalie.'

In a wooden voice Barbara replied, 'She used to ask when you'd be coming.'

Perdita's heart stopped. 'Natalie did?' she asked incredulously.

'Towards the end, yes. But you never came.'

A pang of desolation drove the colour from Perdita's skin. How Luke must hate her, to deny Natalie this one thing! And how dared he play God! The thought of Natalie asking for her in vain hurt some inner part of her soul, marking it with a pain that would never go away.

She said quietly, 'I didn't even know she was ill. We'd lost touch—and no one bothered to tell me.'

Barbara looked unconvinced as well she might. It was an extremely lame explanation.

'I'll finish breakfast,' Perdita said, 'and have a shower, and then if you can help me dress that would be great. Oh—if you could undo my wretched bra first...'

The housekeeper unclipped it, leaving Perdita to eat toast and drink orange juice and coffee without tasting either.

Why, after years of silence, had Natalie wanted to see her? Chewing mechanically, she mulled over various reasons until eventually common sense told her she would never know, so it was useless to worry about it.

Which left her free to transfer her attention to the housekeeper's remark about the girls needing a mother. A mother for the twins would mean a wife for Luke.

Oddly enough, it hadn't occurred to Perdita that he might marry again, but of course he would. Even though his heart was buried with Natalie he was too virile, too potent and compellingly male to stay celibate for long.

Horrified by the fierce, instinctive denial that seared through her, she tried to find a logical reason for her reaction. Of course, if he married again his new wife would become the twins' stepmother, and that was a relationship fraught with possibilities for disaster.

So she had a definite interest in any woman Luke might marry, but for her own peace of mind any inclination to possessiveness would have to be summarily squashed. Although he was the only man she had met who could melt her bones with a look, with the faint scent of his skin, with the brush of his hand on hers, he was not for her. Last night he'd made that obvious.

And in spite of all that, she thought an hour later, showered and dressed in trousers and another silk shirt topped by a woollen jersey, damp hair curling around her shoulders in a flood of pale fire, her swollen foot supported on a footstool in front of her, she would never be anything but an interloper in this house.

Although Bess, the large old Labrador, seemed to have accepted her. She'd certainly given up guarding the house from her and was now lying asleep in a patch of sun, dreaming canine dreams.

One down, four to go, Perdita thought drily. Her eyes wandered around the conservatory. It was the newest part of the house, dating from a year after Natalie had married Luke. When her father had died she'd used part of her substantial legacy to bring in a decorator from Sydney, in Australia, and the conservatory had been his idea.

Perdita could vividly remember Natalie's excitement, as well as the sour remarks from her mother about stupidity and expense. In the space of time from one holiday to the next, the whole house had been completely refurbished, almost all the previous furniture beyond a few pictures and several precious antiques banished to the attics.

Then, Perdita had thought it wonderful, and Natalie's taste impeccable; now, with ten years' exposure to the best the world could offer, she realised that her cousin had been cramped by convention. The homestead had been decorated by an excellent interior designer, and it showed. The furniture was excellent, a superb mixture of antiques and the very best modern, but there were no surprises, none of the quirky little elements that gave a house character and personality.

Pigeon Hill homestead was classical in design and ambience, and the house should have been decorated to go with its timeless elegance, not according to the fashions of a particular decade.

Now it looked dated; even the plants were in decline. Perdita's eyes lingered on the hoya vine twining around an upright. It needed judicious tending; the exquisitely formed icing-sugar flowers in pink and white were as waxy and perfect as ever, the nectar glistening like crystal drops around the stamens, but the leaves showed signs of red spider infestation and lack of fertiliser. And she thought she could see the dreaded cotton wool that indicated woolly aphis.

Pigeon Hill needed overhauling, the garden especially. Natalie had been content with wide lawns and gay borders set in the shelter of magnificent trees planted seventy years before by Luke's great-grandfather, but the whole garden was crying out for a complete redesign, one that accepted the subtropical reality and worked from there.

It was ridiculous that the house should have remained so many years separated from its surroundings by the gravel drive that circled it, even more silly that the only place to sit outside was a tiny bricked terrace which no one ever used. Whatever the season, a sunny day in the north meant gloriously warm weather, days when the sun was hot enough for meals to be taken outside. The Victorians had known that, with their verandas and wide Italianate terraces, made for sitting out.

If she lived here, Perdita thought, rigorously excluding any thought of Luke from her mind, she would enjoy bringing the house and garden into the nineties. Oh, nothing wholesale, although the garden would certainly look vastly different when she'd finished with it. Subtlety was the way to go; the Georgian style of the homestead imposed a formality and balance that would contrast intriguingly with the enthusiastic behaviour of subtropical growth.

She'd love to have the opportunity...

By the time the girls arrived home in the school bus she was heartily bored. They surged noisily into the house, laughing and calling out, but their voices softened as they came towards the conservatory where she was enjoying the afternoon sun. They stood together in the door, not quite shy—more reserved, she thought with a sudden twist of her heart.

'Hello,' she said, smiling. 'Did you have a good day?'

Olivia, the taller one, contented herself with a grave nod and a polite, 'Yes, thank you,' but Rosalind gave her gamine grin.

'We had a spelling test,' she said importantly. 'I got one mistake and Olivia got a hundred per cent.'

'Well done, both of you.' Resisting the urge to ask which word she had misspelt, Perdita put down the magazine she had been reading and said, 'Can you come and talk to me for a while, or do you have to do homework?'

'We have to get changed first and then we have a snack and then we do our homework,' Olivia explained when it seemed as though Rosalind might give in to Perdita's unspoken request for company.

Her sister—the younger by half an hour—said tentatively, 'We could bring our snack and our homework in here, if you like. Daddy said you had an accident in your car last night. What happened?'

'I wasn't looking where I was going,' Perdita told her wryly, 'so I didn't see a car parked on the side of the road just around a corner. I put on the brakes too hard and ended up in the ditch with a sprained wrist.'

'And a sore foot,' Olivia pointed out.

Yes, this one needed accuracy. Like her father, Perdita thought with a contraction of her heart.

'No, that happened when the door opened on to it.' Perdita smiled at them both. 'It's not nearly as bad as it looks. I think Mrs Whittaker likes to practise bandaging.'

Rosalind giggled. 'She's got a first-aid certificate,' she said. 'She used to do the bandages on Olivia and me, and we asked her the questions while she was cooking dinner.'

'Come on, Rosie,' Olivia said, 'we have to go. If Mrs Whittaker says it's all right, we'll bring our homework in here.'

Perdita watched them go with something like pain. How was it possible to love people so dearly when you didn't even know them? Had that week she'd spent with her babies forged indissoluble bonds? For her, anyway, she thought wryly, because clearly it hadn't happened to the girls. Unlike Olivia, Rosalind didn't show any signs of wariness, but clearly neither felt anything but curiosity for their father's guest.

An hour later Perdita was sitting beside Rosalind listening to her read an extract from an encyclopaedia; necessary research for a project on volcanoes. Olivia was at the glass and wrought-iron table working conscientiously at a letter to her grandmother. Through a haze of emotion, Perdita's gaze went from one serious, intent face to the other.

Suddenly Rosalind broke off and bounced to her feet, her face alive with expectancy. 'Daddy's back!' she shouted, dropping the book before racing across to the door.

Olivia followed her more sedately, leaving Perdita infected with the spontaneous excitement that had gripped both girls. Trying to calm her runaway heart, she took a couple of sharp breaths and picked up her magazine, staring down at the page with unseeing eyes.

His voice in the hall filled her with an aching need. He was laughing, and she thought with a swift, sharp pang that she had rarely heard his laughter, even when Natalie was alive. Like Olivia, he had an immense natural reserve; in him it heightened his forceful attraction with a spice of challenge, gave him an edge of danger that was potently attractive.

Risky thinking, she told herself drily.

His step in the hall brought her gaze to the door; deep within her something tight and smouldering burst into flame as he came in, tall, broad, moving with a hunter's predatory grace, his angular face softened by his meeting with his daughters.

You love him, her heart told her mind. You have from the time you were about fourteen, and you're going to love him until the day you die.

'Hello. How's the wrist?' The raw, subtle sexuality of his voice was abated for the moment.

Acutely aware of two pairs of childish eyes on her face, Perdita managed to summon a smile. 'It's improving,' she said. 'Another day or so and it will be much better.'

And then I can go, she should say, but the words wouldn't come. Common sense told her that the longer she stayed at Pigeon Hill the harder it would be for her to make some sort of life for herself without this man and these children, but it was refreshment to her empty heart to be here. She wanted to wring every second of its poignant sweetness.

'She knows a lot about volcanoes,' Rosalind said kindly.

'Ms Gladstone,' he corrected. 'Not she.'

'Perdita,' Perdita said immediately. 'Ms Gladstone sounds like a schoolteacher, and I'm not that.'

Olivia looked at her. 'Perdita sounds like a friend,' she said in a level voice that held more than a ghost of her father's intonation.

'I don't think we know each other well enough to be friends yet,' Perdita said steadily, 'but I'd prefer it if your father would let you call me by that name.'

Her glance met Luke's. After a moment he nodded. 'Very well.'

It was a small surrender, and he knew it, and so, she thought shrewdly, did the girls.

Tugging at her father's hand, Rosalind asked, 'Did you know Perdita had to stand on the edge of a crater in Vanuatu while they took photos of her in a long evening dress? She said it was hot and smelly and the smoke curled around her like a shawl.'

Luke's brows shot up. 'I had no idea modelling could be physically dangerous,' he said sardonically.

'Rarely,' Perdita retorted, 'but occasionally you get power-hungry fashion editors with an eye for the outrageous.' Her tone underlined the words *power-hungry* with delicate mockery. His brows lifted. Glad that the shot had gone home, she resumed, 'Fortunately the shots were excellent. Not like the shoot where I had to hold a large, and thoroughly disgruntled male lion by the mane. I was supposed to look sophisticated and decadent. In the proofs my terror showed through very clearly, and instead of looking noble the lion managed nothing more than frank hunger.'

The girls' eyes widened. Looking down at each fascinated face, Luke sent an unsmiling look at Perdita. I know what you're doing, it said. And with more than a hint of menace, But two can play at that game.

Dropping the girls' hands, he said to them, 'Finish what you're doing while I get changed, and then we'll go out and see to the ponies. I'm glad you're feeling better,' he said distantly to Perdita before he left.

Homework was rapidly done; even the earnest Olivia, Perdita was amused to see, raced through the rest of it. As they packed up she suggested, 'Tell me about your ponies.'

They had one each, both horses of infinite attractions. Olivia's was called Junks, and Rosalind's Crystal. Both girls belonged to the local pony club and rode every Saturday. It was more than obvious that they adored it.

'Do you ride?' Rosalind asked.

Perdita shook her head. 'No.'

'Our mother could ride,' Olivia said quietly. 'Daddy says she had the best seat of anyone he ever knew.'

'Yes.' Perdita's eyes stung. 'When she was on a horse she looked as though she was part of it.'

'When——? Oh, yes, you used to stay up here, didn't you?'

'I started coming up when I was eleven, and after that I came up every holiday until I was sixteen.'

Both children were intrigued. 'What happened then?' Rosalind asked.

What had happened? Just the end of the world.

Perdita said, 'I started to work at a model agency, and before I knew where I was I had a contract to work in Japan. Then my mother died, and after that there wasn't really anything to bring me back to New Zealand.'

'What happened to your mother? Did she die from cancer?' Rosalind asked in a small voice.

'No, darling, not from cancer. She ran across a street in Auckland in the rain and she was killed by a car.'

Luke said, 'All right, you two, are you ready?'

Perdita hadn't heard him come in, and she didn't know what emotions were hiding behind the deep voice and the guarded, hard-honed features. Probably nothing.

'Would you mind if I came and watched?' she asked brightly.

'Can you walk?'

She said, 'Yes. I'll put a pair of boots on.'

Although it was patently obvious that he didn't want her with them, there wasn't much he could say in front of the girls, so she got her way. Her foot was still slightly swollen, but she pulled on a soft pair of suede boots that fitted over the bruise. If there was any mud they were going to be ruined, but what the heck, she thought, she'd sacrifice anything for these precious moments with her children.

And with Luke.

Pinning a smile to her face she went down the stairs and through the house to the back door. Luke waited on the gravel outside, watching with keen eyes as she walked out to the Land Rover.

The horse paddock was not far down the race, which meant, she realised, that the vehicle was for her comfort. It was a pleasant trip through manicured paddocks; the children and Bess sat in the back, the girls discussing something that had happened at school that day, the dog panting, her ears streaming behind as she thrust her head through the window.

In the front the silence was absolute, all-enveloping. Through lowered lashes Perdita watched Luke's hands on the wheel, strong, darkly tanned by a keen sun. Her whole world dwindled, refocused. Those competent hands held her heart without even knowing it. They had the power to be cruel, as cruel as the man himself, yet she couldn't blame him for his savage words of the night before.

She and Luke were linked, uncomfortably united by bonds that would never be sundered, and in spite of the moment of insight in the conservatory, those ties chafed her almost unbearably. Loving a man whose heart was buried in another woman's grave was taking the long, winter road to heartache.

Yet she loved him. All these years she had measured every man she met against him.

Unrequited love might be unfashionable, but it hurt. Of course, he would never allow himself to love her. Unwittingly, she had shattered his image of himself as a faithful husband. Between them they had betrayed Natalie, a betrayal that bit too deep to be exorcised by a decade of exile. He would never forgive her or himself for those maddened moments, even though he now knew they had given him his children.

When they reached the horse paddock Luke parked the Land Rover as close to the fence as he could, and everyone but Perdita piled out, the girls sliding through the palings to offer their ponies pieces of white horse carrot pulled up from the huge farm vegetable garden.

Perdita watched wistfully. Luke's big working horse came up, ignored children, dog and ponies to push his nose into his master's chest, soliciting food, but more, she thought, his affection.

Just like the rest of us. Unbidden, the thought popped into her brain. Luke was the lynchpin, the pivot that everyone revolved around. His children patently adored him, she knew from the past that his staff respected him, he held an important place in the community and she— well, she would have given her life to make him happy.

Which made her insistence on seeing the girls a little paradoxical. She would have died for him, but she was shattering his peace of mind.

It was disturbing to realise that as well as loving him she resented him with an angry bitterness. While she had been exiled, always longing to go back, always aware that for her there could be no return, he had been happy. It was a happiness she couldn't forgive.

That unrecognised resentment had been part of her reason for coming back to Pigeon Hill, but she was truly afraid that it would be love that drove her away again.

'Watch me, Perdita!' Rosalind, of course, as Luke heaved her up on to her pony.

Although she knew they were quite safe, Perdita's fingers clasped tightly together. Luke wouldn't let them do anything dangerous, and even if they fell, helmets protected their heads. Sure enough, when Rosalind began to urge her pony into a gallop, she was stopped by a swift command from her father. Pulling a face, she obeyed.

They looked incredibly confident, but Perdita's knuckles were white by the time Luke called out that it was time to go back to the homestead. It was then that, with a wicked sideways glance at her father, Rosalind set her pony to galloping again. Almost instantly it seemed to trip and Rosalind came hurtling off.

A harsh noise came unchecked from Perdita's throat. She was halfway through the railings when she saw that Luke had got there before her, and was helping the grimacing child up from the soft, muddy ground.

'Do that again,' he said quietly, 'and I'll ground you for a year.'

Rosalind burst into tears. Perdita limped rapidly across the field, her face under such savage control it felt as though she had donned a mask.

'I'm sorry,' Rosalind wept, knuckling her eyes.

'You were showing off.'

'I wanted Perdita to see——'

'You fall off?' he interrupted mercilessly.

Rosalind gulped and blew her nose. 'No,' she said, more fat tears oozing from beneath her eyelids.

He was being far too tough. Now that she could see nothing had happened to the child beyond an assault on her dignity, Perdita mastered the shattering fear that had assailed her, and said peaceably, 'I'm sure she's learned her lesson.'

Luke lifted his head and gave her a steady, inimical glance. Keep out of this, it warned with aggressive, concentrated authority.

Perdita flinched, but managed a conciliatory smile. Surely he was making too much of a fuss? But she remembered the moment of appalling terror as Rosalind had started to slip under the pony's heels, and she too hardened her heart.

'All right,' Luke said, 'we'll talk about it later. Get into the Land Rover.'

He waited until both children had left before asking in a detached voice, 'Are you all right?'

'Yes.'

'You're as white as a sheet,' he said brutally. 'Here, lean on me.'

'No, I'm fine.'

Ignoring her instinctive protest, he put his arm around her shoulder, propelling her across the paddock.

I won't say anything, Perdita promised herself, pretending not to see her daughter's mournful little face as they got into the Land Rover. He's made a good fist of bringing them up so far—but without Natalie's mitigating influence, was he too severe on them?

'When you were riding you looked like Cossacks,' she said to the two girls as Luke strode around the front of the vehicle.

'What's a Cossack?' Olivia asked. Rosalind stopped sniffing.

Perdita told them what she knew of the fabled horsemen of the steppes, handing over to Luke when she ran out of information. When he'd finished imparting his meagre store of Cossack lore, they were back at the house.

Perdita forgot to monitor her walk, and immediately Luke said curtly, 'Wait a moment and I'll help you inside.'

'It looks a lot worse than it is,' she said, smiling to show she meant it.

Without warning he caught her up in his arms, effortlessly carrying her across the gravel.

'Luke, don't be an idiot,' she protested, her voice sharp with dismay. 'You'll pull a muscle in your back or something equally stupid. Put me down!'

'Open the door, Liv,' he said calmly.

Her brow wrinkled, Olivia held the door open. From behind came the sound of Rosalind's giggles. 'Perdita's legs are as long as yours, Daddy,' she said.

Perdita said between her teeth, 'Luke, I can walk, damn it.'

His arms were strong around her; his chest lifted and fell, the pulse at the base of his throat throbbed. A faint hint of sweat tickled her nostrils, sending signals through her receptive body.

'Don't swear in front of the children,' he ordered smoothly.

Both girls laughed. 'Gosh,' Rosalind exclaimed, 'we know all about that. Damn's not really swearing.'

'It is as far as you are concerned,' Luke said, carrying Perdita up the stairs. Both girls followed.

He put her down outside her bedroom. She glowered belligerently at him, but the sight of Olivia's worried face stopped the hot words from tumbling off her tongue. Instead she said lightly, 'Well, if you wake up with a sore back tomorrow morning, don't blame me, OK? You girls are my witnesses. I told him to put me down, didn't I?'

They both nodded. Her frown clearing, Olivia looked from one to the other.

Luke said briskly, 'Stop being shrewish. I lift heavier loads than you every day. Wear slippers until that foot heals. We won't mind, will we, girls?'

'No,' they said, and went through their little ritual once more: fingers linked, name of a poet, and wrinkled brows while they thought up a wish.

Perdita's heart melted. She looked away from Luke's altogether too perceptive scrutiny.

He glanced at his daughters, and for a moment she saw beyond the hard, self-disciplined persona he presented to the world. He loved them with a love she couldn't begin to match, a love that had been years in the making.

Bully for him, Perdita thought, turning to open her door. She had ten years' arrears of love to give, and she'd find a way somehow.

After changing her boots, she limped carefully down to the big room in which the family mainly lived. Conveniently close to the kitchen, it was called the morning-room, but was more like a large, comfortably furnished sitting-room with a dining end to it.

Nothing much had changed there, either, except for a photograph of Natalie in a silver frame. Although her lovely face was marked subtly by the illness that killed her, she smiled out at the world, gallant and cheerful, her blonde hair cut in the gamine style that suited her features so well. Beside the frame two pink camellia flowers glowed in a small crystal vase; it was like a little shrine.

Perdita swallowed and looked around the room. The first time she'd come to Pigeon Hill she had been so accustomed to the confines of a series of city flats that she'd found the multitude of rooms at the homestead utterly confusing, and been astonished that two people could need so many. Pigeon Hill had been built in the days when families were large. There were eight bedrooms and a variety of living-rooms, formal and informal, to carry the entertaining load of a time when guests tended to stay for at least one night, if not a week.

They ate informally in the dining-room. Before going back to her own home to eat with her husband, Barbara had cooked as much as she could of the dinner. All that was left to do was dress the salad and heat the soup.

'No, you don't need to,' Luke said when Perdita offered to help. 'We're experts now, aren't we, girls?'

They certainly were. The girls helped, carrying dishes to the table after they'd set it.

She should enjoy this evening, because she might never see them together like this again; Luke would fight her all the way. Her only weapon was her threat to go to the media, and she couldn't use that too often in case he called her bluff.

Why didn't he understand her need to take some part, however minor, in their lives?

Did he see it as an even further betrayal of Natalie?

Well, Natalie had had them for eight and a half years. She wouldn't have denied Perdita some knowledge of them.

Surely?

'—and she said it would be too hard for me to climb to the top,' Rosalind was saying. 'So I had a go.'

Luke looked at her. 'And did you get there?'

She grinned. 'No, in one place the branches are too far apart, but Liv came up and helped me. I'm going to keep trying until I can do it properly.'

'Just make sure you don't fall,' he said. His gaze flicked across to Perdita, catching her with horror in her eyes. For a moment there was cold, clear condemnation in his gaze, before he looked at his older daughter.

'How did your spelling test go?' he asked.

As Olivia finished her mouthful Rosalind burst into speech.

Luke said, 'I asked Olivia,' and Rosalind fell silent. The older girl said sedately, 'I got them all right.'

Luke smiled at her, that austere self-control warmed by his very obvious affection. Olivia smiled back. Then he switched his attention to Rosalind. It was all very low-key, very—*family* and that was how it stayed for the rest of the evening.

In spite of the tension curling inside her Perdita enjoyed it, although she didn't realise how carefully she watched Luke with his daughters, how closely she monitored the interplay of speech and action and attitude, until they went to bed and she was able to relax.

'Satisfied?' he said when he returned from kissing them goodnight.

She gave him a sharp look.

'That I don't beat them, or crush their innocent little egos, or mentally abuse them.' He crouched to put a log of wood on the fireplace.

Perdita's gaze clung for an electrifying moment to the smooth flexion of muscles in his thighs, the unstudied masculine grace that came from perfect health and fitness.

A quick, savage hunger gripped her, almost smothering the caution she had developed over the years. Dragging her eyes away, she pretended study the watercolour of Pukekukupa painted by a world-famous artist twenty years ago as a thanks offering to Luke's parents who had taken him in and looked after him during a severe bout of influenza.

Perdita knew how much that water-colour was worth; it seemed typical that although the homestead had an excellent security system, and the picture was well lit, it was on the wall of the family living-room rather than in solitary splendour in the drawing-room under spotlights.

'I didn't think you would,' she said calmly.

His smile was humourless. 'No? You certainly spent the evening watching like a hawk.'

She shrugged. 'Part of it was—lack of recognition. I don't think I've ever spent an evening with a family before.'

He made a small sound of disgust. 'What the hell sort of life did you lead?'

An empty one in many ways, ways she was just beginning to understand. Oh, she had filled the days, yet she had kept herself aloof from so much.

Especially children. The loss of her own had wounded her, made her vulnerable, and that wound had never healed.

'I learned a lot,' she said. 'It had its moments.'

'Like the time you danced naked on a tabletop in London?'

A disdainful smile curled her mouth. 'It never happened. Natalie shouldn't have believed everything she read in the scandal sheets,' she said. And because he looked scathing and contemptuous, she added, 'I'll bet she didn't, really.'

'Possibly not. It was the only way she could keep in touch with you. It wouldn't have hurt you to keep in contact.'

'I wrote to her,' she said without expression. 'Several times. She didn't answer, so I gave up.' Some imperative, some hidden need, made her say, 'I wondered whether you'd told her.'

'No,' he said with barely suppressed passion, 'I didn't, God help me. I couldn't.'

Well, she understood that.

'Why didn't you let me know that you were pregnant?' he asked shortly.

Perdita shrugged, staring into the flames. She had been so ashamed, so shocked by his hatred of her, it had simply never occurred to her. Like an animal in pain she had huddled away from the world.

'I didn't think you'd want to know,' she said quietly. 'My mother was furious, of course, and she bustled me into a nursing home. I was quite happy there. She said it was impossible for me to keep the baby, and she was right. And when *it* turned out to be *them*, I knew I didn't have a hope. What good would it have done to tell you?'

'You didn't think I might have felt some sort of responsibility?'

She made a helpless little gesture. 'Possibly, but it was a hopeless situation. If *you'd* known—how could we have kept it from Natalie? I couldn't do that to her.'

'No,' he said. A narrow, sardonic smile twisted his mouth. 'The gods must have found the whole thing bloody amusing. I adopted my own children.'

'I didn't even know that you were thinking of adopting,' she said.

'We'd had our name down for a couple of years. One of Natalie's school friends worked in the social welfare department and she organised the adoption. It was easier because few people wanted twins. Natalie didn't care; she used to say she took one look at them and fell in love.'

'And neither of you suspected?' It seemed impossible to her that they hadn't.

'No, thank God,' he said with such complete conviction that the words fell like heavy stones across her heart.

Swiftly she glanced at her thin gold wristwatch. It was barely nine o'clock. She said, 'I'm glad it was you and Natalie. I used to worry about them—wonder desperately whether they were happy, whether I'd done the right thing. I can see now that they're fine.' She drew a deep breath. Now was as good a time as any to tell him. 'But I'm not going to opt out of their life, Luke.'

He looked up sharply, eyes glittering icily in his cold, angry face. 'You said that you'd see them, then go.'

'I don't think I did.' Bracing herself, she met his gaze steadily, refusing to be intimidated. 'I have no legal rights to them, but I do have moral ones. I don't want to harm them, or upset them, or confuse them, but I want to keep in contact.'

'And if I say no you'll go to the media.' His lip curled. 'Which will almost certainly scar them for life.'

'Only if you're unreasonable,' she said sturdily. 'They are my children, Luke, as well as yours and Natalie's. I carried them for eight and a half months, I spent the last three of those months in bed because they thought I might lose them, I had them in pain and tiredness, I held them and breastfed them for a week because they were small and they needed as good a start in life as they could have, and since then I've never stopped grieving for them. I'm not walking away out of their life as though I never existed.'

CHAPTER FIVE

'SO YOU'RE just going to come exploding into it with all the finesse and impact of a car bomb,' he said in a level voice. 'Eventually they're going to ask who their real parents are. I imagine you won't be able to resist the temptation to tell them, and then they'll realise that their father cheated on their mother.'

Natalie, she thought, and for the first time anger drummed through the word. It was always Natalie!

'From what I've read, that question usually comes in the late teens,' she said, hating her placatory tone. 'Surely if we explained how it happened—that it was a terrible mistake——'

Luke's lean hand clenched slowly into a fist, the involuntary movement all the more powerful for being so slow. His expression made her shrink back into the chair.

'Do you honestly think they'll believe that?' he demanded, scorn echoing harshly beneath the words.

Perdita lifted her chin. 'If neither of us have lied to them before, why shouldn't they believe it? What did you plan to do when they started asking?' she retorted, struggling to sound reasonable rather than furious.

'I was going to help them as much as I could,' he returned abruptly.

'Really?' she drawled.

He shrugged. 'Yes. It was Natalie who hoped that they wouldn't want to know. She said that you never showed any interest in your father's identity.

Only because her mother had made it quite obvious she had no intention of telling Perdita. 'She was wrong. Take it from me, everyone wants to know who their parents are.'

He looked at her keenly. 'Do you know now?'

A humourless smile hardened her mouth. 'Yes. He wasn't all that difficult to find, once I set someone prying.' Her father, the scion of an extremely well-known family, now owned one of the country's largest industrial concerns. For years she had fantasised about finding him, but when she discovered his identity she hadn't tried to contact him. No longer a naïve, unloved child, she understood that for a man like that an illegitimate daughter could be nothing but a nuisance.

'Does he know?' he asked.

She shook her head. 'Why should I tell him?'

'Perhaps he'd like to meet you.'

She laughed cynically. 'Because I've achieved a small measure of fame and money by exploiting my face and body? I doubt whether that would make any difference. He knew my mother was pregnant; he never made any attempt to help her, or get in touch with her. I certainly don't want to have anything to do with him now.'

Luke was watching her with half-closed eyes, the pale translucent gaze oddly opaque. 'He did have a wife and children,' he pointed out.

Perdita's head came up. 'Do you know who he is?'

'Yes.'

A hot, confused sense of betrayal added fuel to her barely repressed anger. 'Natalie, I suppose,' she said acidly.

'Yes.' He paused, looking at her set face, then without haste continued, 'Katherine deliberately set out to destroy his marriage. He was completely infatuated, but her tantrums and hell-bent determination to have her own way soon showed him what sort of life he'd have with her, so he left her and he went back to his wife, who'd been waiting patiently for him to come to his senses.'

'The gospel according to Natalie.' She was horrified by the petty spitefulness of the remark, and said wearily, 'Oh, it doesn't matter.'

He shot back, 'You have to admit that she was a little more objective than Katherine. As it happens, it was your mother who refused to have anything to do with her parents, or take any help from your father. She cut herself off entirely. I imagine her parents were quite glad to get rid of her—she'd been giving them hell for years. But Natalie was soft-hearted, and she kept up the connection.'

Perdita bit her lip. 'Yes, I know,' she said. 'I'm sorry.'

According to Katherine her family had rejected her, yet Perdita didn't disbelieve Luke; her mother was entirely capable of cutting off her nose to spite her face. In fact, it was completely in character for her to do so. Huddled inside the cloak of her pride and fury and wilfulness, blaming everybody but herself for her situation, she'd kept everyone, especially the daughter who had needed her so badly, at a distance.

But that didn't make the man who had fathered Perdita's behaviour any less despicable.

'And just in case you're extrapolating, I don't approve of the way your father turned his back on your mother and his child. I would not have deserted you if I'd known that you were pregnant.'

Suspicion resurfacing, Perdita hesitated. Had Natalie told him that, too? If so, he'd have known that the twins were his children. Had he organised it so that he and Natalie adopted them?

He'd admitted that Natalie had a friend in a position of power in the social welfare department. Had he conspired with her? It would have been so neat and tidy; Natalie couldn't have children, but they were of her family, and they were his. Perhaps she'd been angry that they were girls...

One look at the acutely carved angles of his face told Perdita that she'd never know. Like so much else, the answer was locked in his cold, clever brain.

She drew a shallow, ragged breath. That question was coming to assume a bigger and bigger importance. If he had known of her pregnancy then he had cheated her, taking her children from her as though she'd been nothing but one of his highly bred pedigree cattle. The possibility brought a pang of nausea to her stomach.

Impatient with herself for worrying about something she couldn't change, she said acidly, 'Well, as it happened, everything worked out very well for you, didn't it? It was a pity that I had to come along and inconveniently spoil everything.'

'Damn you to hell,' he said, the words a curse that chilled her soul. 'Why did you come back? To haunt me? You didn't need to come here for that, you've haunted me for years. Or did you just want to throw a spanner in the works?'

'Don't,' she said, anger and suspicion dying in a flood of sympathy. Uncurling her legs, she got to her feet and limped across to lay her hand on his arm. 'It doesn't matter. Don't worry about the girls' reactions; we'll cross that bridge when we come to it.'

The sensuous contrast of her cool fingertips against his heated skin tingled through her and set her heart thudding high in her chest. Swallowing, she stepped backward, but not fast enough; he stopped her swift, instinctive retreat by locking his fingers around her wrist.

'*We*?' he demanded, the angles of his face more pronounced than she had ever seen them. 'There's no future for you here, Perdita.'

'I know,' she whispered, mesmerised by the shifting, glittering ice in his eyes, the way the heavy eyelids narrowed the long eyes, the thin line of his mouth, its beauty held in thrall by anger.

The tension between them increased in quantum leaps as pale eyes met widening green ones.

'Luke?' she said, hardly daring to breathe.

Danger yawned beneath her feet in a gap that pitched dark and perilous, danger that menaced her with pale shards of aquamarine, the faint, evanescent scent of aroused male.

Too late she realised that his frustration and a[...]
were being swallowed up by another emotion, even m[...]
basic, far more physical. And she, heaven help her,
just as hungry, the desire she had kept so firmly
pressed finally unleashed, prowling through her b[...]
implacable, unsparing, concentrated on only one th[...]
gratification.

'*No!*' she said, and whipped her wrist free, tur[...]
and running with scant heed for her sore foot, her h[...]
thundering in a primitive reflex in her throat.

She really thought she had beaten him. She mad[...]
up the stairs, and was almost past his door when
caught her shoulder and whirled her around.

For a moment sheer terror fountained through
the elemental fear of a woman who knew that she
prey, tender meat for a merciless hunter, but even as
looked into that strained face where all pretenc[...]
aloofness had fled to reveal features set in a grim m[...]
of need, the fear evaporated and she fitted herself [...]
his arms with an intense, rapturous joy that had[...]
thing of relief to it.

They had been playing a game, marking te[...]
predator and quarry interchangeable as they
noeuvred, but now the game was over, the cha[...]
ended, the catch was secured in timeless bonds, th[...]
that man cast for woman, woman for man.

His mouth was cruel and demanding as though
wanted to punish her, but with her complete surren[...]
it altered miraculously, conjuring a radiant, seduc[...]
sweetness from some inviolate place hidden so far w[...]
her that no other man had ever been able to read[...]

Perdita gave him all he asked for, everythin[...]
wanted, so ensnared by the piercing enchantment of
moment that she had no conception of caution, or [...]
dence, or defending herself. When he picked her up
barely noticed, for her clamouring senses were o[...]
taken by the dangerous security of his arms around
the rapid tattoo of his heart beneath her cheek.

But the slight roughness of carpet on her feet broke the spell, and into her dazed mind there crept some sort of recognition. They were in his room, yet this wasn't the room she remembered.

However, nothing had changed except the bed. The brass bedstead Natalie had loved was gone. In its place stood an old, wooden four-poster of mellow wood, polished by the years and loving care. It looked incongruous in the blue and white and gold room Natalie had decorated so painstakingly with cherubs and watercolours and drifts of silk.

'I had it brought down from the attic,' Luke said, as though he understood.

Somehow that simple statement banished all Perdita's qualms. Smiling, her lashes drooping, she reached up and kissed him with all the fervour and desire she'd dammed for so long.

Only this man, she thought as she drowned in white-hot sensation, only ever this man.

'Perdita,' he said huskily, his voice deep and thick and shaken, 'how long have you been waiting for this? Aeons, like me? No, you've been filling your life very satisfactorily, haven't you, with your work and your lovers?'

'It doesn't matter,' she said softly, stopping the words with a finger. 'Nothing matters but this, this place, you.'

He burned comfort away in a kiss that rocked the foundations of her soul. Sighing, Perdita welcomed him into her mouth. Her body tensed, readying itself for him; heat curled through her veins, pulsed at innumerable pleasure points, ached at the fork of her body in a longing that would no longer be denied.

As he drew her down on to the bed she understood at last what she had hungered for during the lost years: the evocative scent of his passion, the heat and strength of his body, the primitive magic of the way they fitted together, the arousing weight of his hand on her breast as he shaped its contours with something like reverence.

At this moment he was hers as much as she was his;
the conventions, the situation they found themselves in,
everything forgotten in the consuming flood of fire. At
this moment he no longer measured every woman in
Natalie's frame, and neither did Perdita remember that
her cousin was engraved on his heart.

At this moment, a man and a woman free of the past's
shackles, they came together in an embrace as old as
time, as fresh as tomorrow.

Perdita shivered when his fingers skimmed the tight
little peak in the centre of her breast. Suddenly, as though
the flimsy barrier of her shirt was too much for him, he
yanked sharply at the silk, ripping the buttons free of
their holes, bending his head to close his mouth over the
thin soft net of her bra while his hand unclipped it from
behind.

Instinctively her back arched, bringing her up against
the hard wall of his chest. She fumbled at the fastenings
of his shirt, but her hand was lax, without strength, and
she muttered, 'I want—I want—damn it, I can't——'

He lifted his head, and she almost cried out as the
heated suckling ceased and a chill drove her nipple into
painful sensitivity. A smile as fierce and unrelenting as
the passion that coloured the savage sweep of his cheek-
bones drew the skin taut over the magnificent frame of
his face.

'What do you want?' he asked through his teeth. 'Tell
me, Perdita. I'll give you anything you want, everything
you want, so much that you'll never need to want again.
Just tell me, and you can have it.'

'Your shirt.' She looked at him with glazed eyes, her
mouth tender and slightly swollen, her hands fluttering
ineffectually against the front of his shirt.

'Do you want me to take it off?'

Swallowing, her throat parched, she nodded.

He laughed deep in his throat. 'Then you must take
yours off, too. I've often wondered what you'd look like
as you took your clothes off for me. Venus rising above

the foam, Eve in innocent abandon, Helen in all her glory... Let me see you undress, Perdita, just for me.'

She sat up, her hands shaking as she pulled at the buttons of her cuff. Sudden pain in her wrist set a small frown between her brows, but she kept trying, in thrall to the compulsion that drove her towards some distant goal, a goal she didn't even recognise.

'Hell,' he said sharply, 'I'd forgotten. No, let me...'

He stripped the shirt from her so solicitously, so tenderly, that tears blurred her eyes. Then he took his own shirt off, and she swallowed again, silenced by the sheer size of him, the bronzed skin of his shoulders and chest, the masculine pattern of coppery hair across his chest that arrowed down in the most suggestive way to his belt, the tiny nipples that stood proud against the sleek skin.

'We're so different,' he said quietly, seeming to understand her need to look, to come to terms with his size. 'And yet we fit so well.'

The startling contrast in colour between his hand and the pale curve of her breast was a pagan reminder that he spent much of his life working outside.

'You look like something rare and special under the moon,' he murmured, his eyes taking in her enchanted face, the clear transparency of skin across her shoulders and breast, warmed already by rising heat. 'Some fierce Celtic goddess, demanding worship as well as love. Or a nymph in ancient Greece, perhaps, and I'm the satyr.' His smile was edged, almost sardonic. 'That's how I've always felt about you, that I took you and ravished you, and made my own punishment...'

Unable to concentrate because his touch was summoning forth an intense rapture, a potent fiery, mindlessness, she stroked his cheek. It burned beneath her hand.

'Hush,' she said, and bent her head to close her lips around one of the unfamiliar peaks in his breast.

He shuddered, and suddenly there was no time for thought, no space for anything but this wild, devouring fever. She never remembered how the rest of their clothes came off; she only knew that she was lying on the bed, shadowy sheets and pillows beneath her, their percale like clouds against her sensitised skin, and he was with her, that lean, big body poised and threatening above her.

Smiling, she moved her legs in invitation, and he slid his hand down, kissing her throat as his finger searched and found the tiny source of her passion. She moaned into his mouth, and once more her back arched in that convulsive, unspoken invitation.

'Yes,' he said hoarsely, 'yes, that's it, that's it. Like fire and splendour and bounty, clinging to me——'

He waited, but she whimpered her need, pulling him down, on to her, into her, and in one deliberate thrust he filled her entirely, his chiselled face intent and unsmiling, his eyes glittering with a passion that invoked an answering response. Even as he began to move she crested and fell into rapture, waves of ecstasy robbing her of anything but the blind need to surrender to the rhythm that rose from her deepest being.

Instantly he moved again, driving deeper and deeper, taking over her body entirely, forcing her further and further beyond the mundane into some unrecognised place until she cried out, her voice shaking with unbridled emotions, so far removed from the woman she had always considered herself to be that her disorientation was complete.

She felt the sudden stiffening of his body, strength gathering to his need, and then his head was flung backwards and he spilled into her.

Perdita went with him, hands gripping his shoulders, the lithe, honed length of her acceptant of his merciless possession as though this was what she had been born for.

He came down slowly and, smiling, unthinking, unworried, content at that moment as she had never been before, she held his beloved weight in her arms.

After a while he stirred. Murmuring a soft protest, she linked her hands across his broad back.

'It's all right,' he said, his voice still thick with satiation. He rolled on to his side, scooped her up and pulled her to lie across his shoulder.

Bones robbed of strength, she lay relaxed and inert across him, aware of the tangy scent of mingled sweat as it dried, the scent of passion heavy in the quiet room.

'I want you to marry me,' he said, his voice reflective and detached.

Instantly Perdita's slumbrous peace vanished. She lifted her head to stare at him, eyes straining as the colour ebbed from her face. 'What?'

'You heard.'

If there had been any emotion in his voice, anything but splintered ice in his eyes she would probably have said yes there and then, but although the words hovered temptingly on her tongue she knew she couldn't.

'Why?' she asked, trying to pull away. 'You were protecting me, so I'm not likely to get pregnant this time.'

'That's not it, and you know it,' he bit out.

'What is it, then? And don't try to tell me that you think it would be best for the girls. They don't know me.'

'They're eager to welcome a mother.' A lean finger tipped her chin up so that he could see her face. 'What's the problem? Don't you want to see them grow up? I thought that was why you came here.'

'Damn you, don't you use my children against me,' she whispered furiously.

Gone was the fiercely tender lover; Luke was now her enemy, determined to get his own way. 'I'll use whatever I have to,' he said. Her body sprang to life beneath seeking, experienced fingers. 'And you've given me such a lot of ammunition, my beautiful, fiery, seductive, sexy Perdita.'

He bent to kiss her breast. At least, that was what she thought he was going to do. Steeling herself for the powerful sorcery of his mouth, she was shocked when he found the small dimple of her navel and explored it with his tongue.

'Stop it,' she gasped, appalled at the intensity of her response.

She felt his smile against the smooth skin, and desire stirred languorously in the pit of her stomach. Amazingly, he too was becoming aroused.

She groaned, 'No, you can't—not yet.'

'Your other lovers must have been pretty effete,' he taunted. 'Touch me, Perdita—feel for yourself whether I can or not.'

She turned her face away, closing her eyes, shutting out the sight of him, trying to block out her own surging, unmanageable response.

He laughed in his throat, and ran a possessive hand down her leg, fondling the slender bones of her ankle, the fine, high arch of her foot. Perdita had never been touched like this before; she held her breath, especially when his fingers sought the bruise where the door had opened on to it.

'It looks painful,' he said, and kissed the discoloured flesh.

'Don't.' Her stomach knotted with need and astonishment.

'Why not?' The deep words lingering against her skin brought it out in gooseflesh. 'I did it, I should kiss it better. That's how it works, you know.'

'Luke, I don't want you kissing my feet.'

He laughed again, but came up beside her again, his hand resting against the shaking, thudding place where her heart threatened to burst free from her body.

'Why not?' he mocked softly, amusement mingling with a satisfaction she reacted to with helpless anger. 'How modest you are, Perdita. Was it so easy to keep your other lovers at bay? I'm not so easily managed. I intend to kiss you everywhere, every silken, scented inch of your skin, every long, supple limb, until I know you so well by touch that I'll be able to find my way around you in the darkest night. And if you think that the missionary position is the only one for making love, I'll have infinite pleasure in changing your mind.'

Her skin blazed with colour, a tide that ran like fire through her entire body. Dumbly she shook her head.

'Yes,' he said, and there were generations of dominant male in his tone, a concentrated purposefulness that sent chills down her spine. 'Make up your mind, Perdita. You're going to marry me—you know it as well as I do.'

It would be so easy to yield, so simple, yet she was intensely suspicious of this abrupt about-face. Luke didn't make decisions like this. He was too sensible, too intelligent, too pragmatic, to hitch his future to a whim.

'Was it something I said?' she asked harshly.

He looked amused. 'No.'

'Then what made you change your mind? What changed me from being the eager adolescent who was so hot for her cousin's husband that she crawled into his bed and had her wicked way with him, and the unnatural mother who came back ready to turn her children's life into turmoil so she could satisfy her belated maternal instincts? Apart from the sex, of course.'

'Perhaps I got sick of fighting it,' he said, his temper surfacing.

'It?'

'The sex, as you so charmingly call it. This—attraction, fascination, sorcery, whatever it is. And don't tell me you don't know what I'm talking about. It's been there ever since the summer you turned seventeen. I took one look at you and wanted you, and you wanted me, even though we both tried to ignore it. Eleven years hasn't managed to kill it, so we might just as well give in.'

At the flat, unemotional tone a hope she hadn't even recognised died stillborn. He resented this physical thralldom just as much as she did. A bad basis for a marriage, but perhaps the only one that would enable him to marry again. After all, if your heart was buried in your dead wife's grave anything other than lust would be faithlessness.

Perdita knew herself too well; eventually, if she gave in, she'd come to hate him, because she wanted everything: love, not lust, tenderness instead of chivalrous consideration, a passion so intense he forgot to use that immense expertise and lost himself as completely as she did in the moment. She wanted the whole banquet, not just the crumbs from Natalie's table.

She was still shaking her head when he bent and put his mouth to the flat plane of her stomach.

'It won't make any difference,' she said, pressing her lips together to keep back the betraying little gasps. 'I'm not stupid enough to be seduced into something I know will be bad for me.'

'I've always loved a challenge.' He kissed the place where her hip jutted, biting gently into the smooth skin, looking down with satisfaction when colour rushed into the small indentations made by his teeth. 'Why would it be so bad for you, Perdita?'

'Because lust has to be about the worst reason for marriage.'

He lifted his head and looked down at her desperate face, his own suddenly withdrawn and aloof, the bony framework forbidding beneath the bronzed skin. 'But we have much more than lust to share. We have two daughters,' he said, stroking from her stomach to her breast with his free hand, halting just short of the curve of her breast so that she could have cried out with frustration.

'I suppose I shouldn't be surprised that you're prepared to use them to get your own way,' she said wildly.

His expression took on an oddly reckless aspect, but that maddening hand kept its whisper-soft travelling, sending unbearably dangerous messages to her brain.

'They're what it's all about, surely. But you're not really all that interested in them, are you?' he said with cool calculation, his eyes unsparing as they searched her face. 'You really don't want to do any of the work of bringing them up. You want to be the parent who spoils them, then, when you get sick of them, you'll send them back to me.'

'*No!*'

'Then tell me, Perdita, why you won't marry me. Make me understand.'

The sound of her heart was the only noise in the taut, tempting silence. Oh, she could tell him all right. Just watch his face as she said, I love you too much to marry you like this, and see him back off with humiliating speed.

Love implied responsibility for another's happiness, and he wouldn't want that. He wanted a mistress to take to bed every night, a hostess, a mother for his children, a woman who would never touch him emotionally, leaving his memories of Natalie inviolate, like a shrine in his heart.

No, she wouldn't tell him. She didn't trust him not to use her love as a weapon. Where he was concerned she was perilously weak, far too vulnerable.

Wrenched by pain, she said quietly, 'It wouldn't work and you know it. Marriage is a chancy enough thing when people fall in love; it would have no hope of succeeding with us.'

'I think you're wrong.' Although he stopped his tormenting stroking, he stayed where he was, looking down at her so that he could see every movement of every muscle in her face, every revealing, reluctant reaction. 'Most marriages fail because one or both doesn't understand what's expected of them. We'd know. And this——' he bent to kiss the slope of her shoulders, not lifting his head until she was shaking with desire '—this is good. It will last.'

'I won't be manipulated,' she said brusquely, summoning anger to help her because logic didn't seem to be getting her anywhere.

'I'm merely pointing out one of the benefits. That's not manipulation. You must have been a pretty good businesswoman, Perdita, to have done as well as you have. Surely you can see the advantages.'

'For you, perhaps,' she said angrily.

'For the children as well. They need a mother.'

'Barbara,' she muttered, refusing to admit defeat.

'She does her best, but she's got her own life to lead. They need a mother, not a housekeeper. There'd be advantages for everyone, Perdita. After all, that's why you came here, wasn't it, to see your children? That's why you decided to ignore the document you signed, because just seeing them wasn't enough, you needed to know more about them? If you marry me you'll occupy the most important place in their lives.'

With an effort of will she didn't think she was capable of, she pushed herself up on her arm. 'Luke, don't. I want to go to my own room.'

He must have heard the raw edge of fear in her tone for he looked at her searchingly. 'Of course,' he said after a moment. 'Wait, I'll get you something to wear.'

He went into the dressing-room and came out with a flamboyant silk robe. Even in her state of shock Perdita looked at it with raised eyebrows.

'A birthday present from a cousin who thought I was becoming too staid,' he said, reading her thoughts. He wrapped the bright silk around her, avoiding her sore wrist, and stood, apparently unconcerned at his nudity.

'Think over what I suggested,' he said, holding her gaze with his own. 'I think we could be very happy together.'

The ardent, elemental lover had been replaced by the man of compelling power and authority. Watching him shrug into a sober dressing-gown that suited him much better, Perdita wondered what it would need to break permanently through that distant, maddening self-sufficiency.

Natalie, she thought wearily. And she wasn't Natalie, never would be.

'Come on, I'll see you back to your room,' he said.

Typical Luke, she thought wearily once she was safe in her own bed, staring with wide, unseeing eyes at the ceiling. He'd been brought up properly; after making love with a woman you always escorted her back to her room just in case something nasty was lying in wait along the hall.

Yet in spite of those excellent manners, Luke was as primitive as the most barbaric of invaders. He had buried his heart in Natalie's grave, and now he was going to be practical. Marrying Perdita would mean he didn't need to worry about a wife who was unable to get on with his daughters.

And she had been trained by Natalie; the holidays she had spent at Pigeon Hill had been like a course at a finishing school. With that bedrock of good manners firmly in place, the ten years spent mixing with the rich and famous could only be an asset. Pigeon Hill had always been noted for its hospitality; anyone who was anyone in New Zealand eventually ended up there, and many of the important overseas visitors.

No doubt Luke would be pleased to have a wife with such good social training.

Especially as they made potent sorcery in bed together. Luke was a sexual athlete, his body as keenly honed for the transmission of pleasure as though he trained specially for it, and when he touched her all hope of common sense flew out of the window.

But there was more to marriage than being an excellent hostess and making love, more than being a mother.

Reluctantly, she recalled the man she'd had an affair with two years after she had left New Zealand. In a way she had loved Howard very much, but when he'd finally managed to persuade her into his bed she'd experienced

nothing beyond a mild pleasure, certainly none of the
fierce incandescence she'd felt in Luke's arms.

Howard hadn't been able to cope with her lack of response, seeing it as some sort of slur on his manhood.
Very soon Perdita had decided that they were going nowhere, and in spite of his objections had broken with
him. She still felt wretched when she thought of his pleas
for time, his promise to do better, as though it was his
fault! Still, he hadn't grieved for long; within a few
months he'd married another model. Unfortunately, that
hadn't lasted either. In less than two years they were
divorced.

Some months later Perdita ran across him at a party
and listened with a patient ear while he tried to explain
what went wrong.

'We got married because there was this powerful pull,
this white-hot attraction between us both, and I thought
that was what I wanted, but instead I got lumbered with
another person's life. She was obsessed with me,' he said
tiredly. 'God, Perdita, have you any idea what that's like?
I felt trapped, and I couldn't get away because it would
have killed her.'

He gloomed into his drink. 'Every time we had a row
she'd be broken. I'm not normally a cruel man, and I
couldn't bear to hurt her, but in the end it was too much.'

'Where is she now?'

He looked haggard. 'She's trying to pick up the pieces
of her life. So am I.'

Intensely sorry for both of them, Perdita took heed
of the warning. Sex could be wonderful, desire almost
irresistible, but it was not enough to keep a marriage
together.

Yet, thought her mind in sly subversion, if she married
Luke they would have so much more in common than
lust. The children, for one. And she could make a good
life for herself at Pigeon Hill.

Restlessness drove her from the bed. Pulling the curtains back, she stared out. The moon bestowed enough

light for the crouching clumps of totara and puriri trees to show up boldly above the grass. The dark bulk of Pukekukupa loomed stark against the sky, the domed, branchy tops of its ancient kauri fringing the horizon. The massive trees grew quickly at first and then settling down into a slow, infinitely patient expansion for hundreds of years. Only two centuries ago Northland had been full of them, vast areas of enormous trees.

Once Natalie and Luke had taken her further north to the home of friends, and on the way they had passed an area where a petrified forest stood. Aeons before, a huge forest had stood there, serene and inviolable, until in an instant some unspeakable catastrophe had brought the sea rushing in, toppling and drowning the forest before receding.

An earthquake, perhaps? There were very few in Northland, and those usually light, but perhaps there had been a bad one. Or a tsunami; had White Island in the Bay of Plenty erupted and sent walls of water rushing northwards? Probably not; in modern times any tidal waves that hit New Zealand's coast were low and not in the least dangerous because they had been set off by earthquakes off South American coasts.

Perhaps an asteroid had splashed down, she thought, breathing in the fresh, pure air, the one that some scientists considered might have destroyed the dinosaurs.

Life was cheap. Earth took little notice of the doings of mankind; if humanity was wiped out tomorrow, the planet would shrug its shoulders and eventually some other life form would become the dominant species.

It should make her feel that her own problems were very small.

Intellectually it did, but her heart was where the pain was, and philosophy wasn't any help to that. Shivering, she walked across the carpeted floor and got back into her warm bed, pulling the duvet around her shoulders. She wriggled her wrist experimentally. It still hurt like hell when she moved it too far.

She should never have come. She should have listened to the warnings of prudence, warnings in which *risk*, and *danger*, and *pain* had figured largely.

She smiled tenderly, warmly, into the darkness. What element of risk could weight the balance against the joy of meeting her daughters, the poignant bittersweet delight of discovering that she loved Luke with all her heart?

Perhaps when she left Pigeon Hill he would realise that he felt more for her than a straightforward, convenient passion. She could only hope so, anyway, because although she seemed doomed to love him, she wasn't going to marry him until he had consigned Natalie to the past. That was too great a risk.

Waking early, she decided to go down for breakfast rather than have Barbara bring her tray up again. As she got into her clothes—going without a bra, and donning a cashmere jersey without buttons and trousers that zipped up easily—she listened to the early morning noises of the house.

Luke's voice, firm yet affectionate when he called the twins from their respective bedrooms, was almost immediately replaced by theirs, just too distant for her to make out the words. Outside in the silver-white flowers of a michelia tree a thrush lifted its speckled breast to the polished sky and poured out its heart in song. Down by the vegetable garden a huge jacaranda stood guard over a row of cherry guava bushes. As Perdita watched, several magnificent native pigeons, or kukupa, flew in from the bush on Pukekukupa, white breasts gleaming in the sun, and settled with considerable fuss into the sheltering branches of the jacaranda.

Ten years ago twenty or thirty of the big birds used to come regularly to plunder the cherry guavas. Last night over dinner they had discussed its rapid slide towards extinction, a vicious downwards spiral caused by the ravagement possums had wrought in the bush, and in Northland the depredations of poachers.

'I thought they were completely protected, like all native birds,' Perdita had said.

Olivia nodded. 'They are, but it doesn't stop people from shooting them.'

'Have any poachers shot over Pukekukupa?' Perdita asked.

Luke sent her a warning look. 'A couple of weeks ago I was looking for a wild boar in the reserve and found a pile of feathers under a tree,' he said grimly. 'There certainly aren't nearly as many birds as there used to be. They're not dangerous, pigeon poachers, just greedy and uncaring.'

And he had very firmly changed the subject. Obviously he didn't want the girls worried.

Even paradise had its ravishers. Perdita glowered out of the window. It hurt to think of people shooting the glorious, trusting birds. In some hidden part of her she had always assumed that Pigeon Hill would continue to be as it was in her memories, idyllic, unaffected by time or events, where the sun always shone and there had been love and laughter, and she had been valued.

Her life had been so bleak and circumscribed until Natalie married and came to live here. After that there had been the holidays to look forward to, a keen, childishly vivid anticipation to flavour the reality of living with an embittered mother. Coming to Pigeon Hill had been like coming out of biting cold into the radiant warmth of a summer's day. No wonder she loved the place.

But that was then, and this was now. If she came to live here, would she be disappointed with the mundane flavour of life on a cattle and sheep station?

No, she thought as she walked back along the silent hall from the bathroom. The serenity and quiet rhythms of country life, the instinctive, immutable response to the seasons, to the weather, satisfied some part of her that had been lonely and unfulfilled during the busy years. Not that she'd been conscious of pining—wherever she'd been she'd managed to keep herself reasonably cheerful, but here she wouldn't have to try.

She hesitated at the top of the stairs, wondering just how she was going to deal with Luke. Still, putting it off wouldn't make it any easier. Summoning all of her self-discipline, she walked down, realising that the bruising in her foot had eased.

'I did it, I should kiss it better,' Luke had said last night. 'That's how it goes.'

It seemed that such primitive magic worked.

Perdita had spent years of her life assuming expressions for various photographers. She put one on now, an air of serene nonchalance, of sophisticated composure. Nevertheless, colour crept through her skin as she walked into the morning-room and smiled impartially around.

'Good morning,' Luke said, getting to his feet, his pale eyes resting mockingly on the clear peach-pink of her blush.

She distributed a greeting between him and the girls, her heart swelling as they smiled back, Olivia for once forgetting her caution.

'Did you sleep well?' Luke asked, a note in his voice reminding her of what had happened the night before.

Keeping her lashes lowered, she sat down. 'Very well, thank you,' she said primly.

Fortunately Barbara Whittaker bustled in, saying as soon as she came through the door, 'Oh, you didn't need to get up, you know. I was going to take a tray up.'

Smiling, Perdita answered, 'I'm an early riser, so I thought I'd save you the trouble.'

'It's no trouble,' the older woman said.

The girls were looking at Perdita with frank interest, Rosalind smiling around her toast, Olivia with the grave poise that was so much a part of her.

'Are you going to stay here for long?' Rosalind asked with artless candour. At Olivia's frown she said defiantly, 'Well, I want to know.'

'It's rude,' Olivia said sternly. She explained, 'Rosie doesn't mean to be rude, she just never stops to think.'

'Perdita knows that,' her sister said cheerfully. 'Are you staying long, Perdita?'

'No, I have to go back to Auckland.' Perdita refused to meet Luke's eyes as she accepted a glass of orange juice from him. She was being cowardly bringing her decision into the open in front of the girls, where he couldn't use any of his battery of weapons against her, but common sense told her that she was in a better position to make it stick by doing just that.

She felt the fore of his attention like a swift lance. 'Not until that wrist is better,' he said calmly, offering her some toast. 'You won't be able to drive for more than fifteen minutes before it starts to hurt.'

'Oh, I'll be all right,' she said lightly.

His voice was perfectly smooth, almost bland, but there was no mistaking the unyielding finality of his words. 'You'd better let a doctor make the decision,' he said, handing over a small pottery bowl of marmalade. 'Until then, you can stay here. We are accustomed to visitors, aren't we, Rosie, Olivia?'

Perhaps she had been foolish to bring the girls in on this. Perhaps he was punishing her for it. One glance at their alert young faces as they agreed enthusiastically that yes, they were definitely accustomed to visitors, and she realised she couldn't tell him to go to hell.

She allowed her eyes to narrow, but the smile he gave her was as bland as his voice. 'That's settled, then,' he said. 'Would you like to pour yourself some coffee? Or Barbara can make tea if you prefer it?'

'No, coffee will be fine,' she said automatically.

'Good. I'll be home today, so you won't be lonely. I'm going to check out the back fences, so you can come with me in the Land Rover, if you like.' He spoke as though offering a treat to an especially well-behaved child.

Fuming, her emotions held barely in check, she said tonelessly, 'What fun! Thank you.'

CHAPTER SIX

ALTHOUGH the wind blew keenly from the west, the day had a burnished, sparkling perfection that couldn't help but raise Perdita's spirits. Settled into the Land Rover after breakfast, Bess and two farm dogs ensconced in the back with identical expressions of alert, intelligent interest, Luke driving along the narrow metalled track that ran from the front of the farm to the back, she had to fight the dangerous well-being that flooded her. The memory of what had happened the night before burned like a beacon at the back of her brain, but for the moment a hard-won serenity prevailed.

'There have been enormous changes in farming since you were last here,' Luke observed, speaking with cool detachment as though to a casual visitor. 'The country's gone through a recession, of course.'

'How have things been for you?' She shouldn't ask, but she needed to know.

His sideways look held mockery and another, more equivocal emotion. Betraying desire clutched her entrails, turned her bones to liquid.

'We've managed,' he said. 'I'm lucky, of course; I don't have any debt on the place. A reasonable number of the conventional, steady, stick-in-the-mud farmers have come through in reasonable shape. Some of the entrepreneurs managed to hang in, but too many good farmers and most of those in it for the money lost their shirts.'

'Tell me what's been happening,' she said.

'Didn't you keep in touch with events in your own country?'

Although no note of censure sounded in his voice she replied stiffly, 'I did my best, but New Zealand is a tiny

115

country in the scheme of things. It's hard to get news, especially when you're in darkest Europe.'

And there had been no one to keep her up-to-date. While in the nursing home she had lost touch with her school friends, and after the lack of any answer to the tentative letters she'd written to Natalie, there had been no one else.

She wondered now whether any of those letters had reached her cousin. The mail was delivered to the homestead by the odd job man who dropped it off at the office, so Luke always had first look at it. It would have been simple for him to confiscate any letter from her.

Yet another thing she'd never know, she thought with a fleeting look at Luke's arrogant profile. That obdurate silence had hurt her unbearably. She had wanted so much to keep in touch, to feel that even though she could never go back to Pigeon Hill she had roots somewhere.

During the long, lonely years of exile, every time she read about New Zealand she mourned for her children, recalled the hopelessness of her feelings for the man beside her. After a while it had been easier to take only the most superficial interest.

She listened as he spoke, partly seduced by the raw silk texture of his voice, until she was lost in his words. He had a sharp, incisive mind that gave no quarter; although Perdita had done reasonably well at school, she hadn't worked hard. Natalie was fond of saying that she'd learned nothing at school, and Perdita had unconsciously absorbed her philosophy.

It had been another source of tension between her and her mother. Katherine had never ceased to point out that a woman with no qualifications had no future in this world, no prospects, especially if she was stupid enough to saddle herself with an illegitimate child.

Perdita had preferred to listen to Natalie, who told her she didn't need to go to university, there would always be a place for her if she was amusing and kind-hearted and charming. Her love of reading would give her all the education she needed.

Unconsciously, because she could never remember coming to any decision, Perdita had assumed that the place would be with Natalie; she'd been, she thought now with a haunted little smile, very naïve.

Looking back, she suspected that she'd been punishing Katherine by refusing to do the one thing that might have pleased her mother. It was only in the last few years that she had realised just how much she had missed, and deliberately set out to catch up. Listening to Luke as he dissected the turmoil the country had endured during the time she had been away, she was glad she had.

She began to ask questions, and before long they were discussing modern economic theory. It surprised her that with so much left unsaid, so much between them, the conversation should move smoothly, punctuated now and then by muffled barks from the dogs as they saw something exciting through the windows.

The land looked in excellent heart. In paddocks coloured the deep green that indicated fertility and loving care, the cattle were sleek beneath the winter sun, lifting their heads in mild surprise as the Land Rover went past.

From economics the conversation slid on to new methods of farming, taking an abrupt turn when Luke observed that he was halfway into organic farming.

That of course led to ecology; she discovered that he was on the board of one of the country's biggest conservation movements, and just back from the first world summit on the subject in Brazil, about which he was cynically hopeful.

Stealing a look at the strong face starkly outlined against the umbrageous crown of a puriri tree, Perdita thought that he was so much more than a merely charismatic man, relying on natural magnetism and inherited wealth to get by. Over the years she had met many such, superficially sophisticated and spoilt, and quickly learned to discern the essentially shallow man beneath the slick, glossy surface.

Luke was different; a complex, disturbing man, hard-edged and disciplined, yet able to love. However, that ability to love, she thought, recalling his reaction to Rosie's disobedience the evening before, didn't mean that he was permissive or indulgent.

She said, 'You were awfully abrupt with Rosie when she galloped last night.'

She expected to be told to mind her own business, but he said calmly, 'Do you think I should have let her keep on galloping? Bareback, with no reins?'

'Well, no, but she——'

'Rosie is impetuous and a show-off. She needs to learn that her actions have consequences.'

She looked at him, saw an unyielding profile and said on a sigh, 'The girls are lucky.'

That surprised him. He directed a narrowed glance sideways.

'They're obviously very secure,' she explained, re-membering her own mother, who hadn't cared enough to set limits on her behaviour. 'They know you love them.'

'They were secure in Natalie's love, too,' he said harshly.

'Yes, I can tell.'

With that mysterious intuition he seemed to possess, he said, 'Have you rethought your decision of last night?'

'No,' she said, projecting as much determination as she could into her voice.

'There's no hurry.'

His tone and expression were so non-committal that indignation as well as pain jagged through her. Of course she'd known that he didn't really want to marry her, but he might at least have made some pretence.

No, she was being utterly idiotic. The last thing she wanted him to do was lie to her. She was strong enough to accept the truth.

However unpalatable it might be.

At last they arrived at the length of fence he wanted to check; half an hour sitting side by side, she thought as the Land Rover drew to a halt, and neither had made any reference to their lovemaking last night. Yet not a look or word had been unaffected by it. They were somehow linked, linked as they hadn't been when she had conceived the twins, because then the lovemaking hadn't been for her.

It all came back to Natalie.

Guilt and love and longing. Betrayal and love, despair and anger and grief so tightly wound together nothing could separate them...

Last night she had dreamed that Luke loved her, that he had relinquished Natalie's cherished ghost and turned from the past to face the future, yet even as the images formed in her sleeping brain she had known it to be pure illusion, the product of a wishful heart. The sooner she could accept that, the better it would be for her. Only now did she understand that part of the reason she had come back to Pigeon Hill was that in some very well-hidden corner of her mind hope still lurked.

That Luke had deliberately tried to make sure she never discovered where her children were should have shown her how empty and unattainable that forlorn hope was. Oh, she could understand his reasons; Perdita didn't relish explaining to an older Rosalind or Olivia—especially Olivia—how she came to be conceived adulterously.

But that didn't excuse his behaviour. She knew how deeply a lack of knowledge of one's family history could wound, and he had deliberately courted that pain for his daughters.

'Do you want to get out?' Luke asked, opening his door. He gave a concise order and both the farm dogs leapt on to the grass. Bess followed more slowly, as befitted her greater age and dignity.

'Yes, of course.' Without thinking Perdita went to unclip the seatbelt, only to be stopped by a sharp jab of pain from her wrist.

'I'll do that,' Luke said crisply, clicking it free.

Perdita looked up, arranging her expression into one of poised composure. It was difficult to sustain when she met his eyes, cold and clear as ice, the pale translucence not hiding an inexorable determination. A shiver of foreboding threaded its way through her cells.

'It's no use,' he said, watching her with the uncanny, terrifying patience of a hunter so attuned to his prey that he understood the thoughts forming in its head. 'You can struggle all you like, but I've got you trapped in the oldest cage of all, and you can't ever get free because you made the bars.'

'Sex might be enough for you,' she said quietly, 'but it's not for me.'

He reached into the back to pick up a hammer and some staples. Straightening up, he said, 'If all I wanted you for was sex I'd make you my mistress,' adding with an undertone of hardness, 'After all, you're accustomed to that role. But it's not just the sex, transcendental though that is.'

'I'm not accustomed to being a mistress,' she bit out. 'I'd find it utterly demeaning to be kept by a man.'

'Don't change the subject.'

'In fact,' she said, eyes glittering with anger, 'that's what I'd be if I married you, because the only reason for a couple to marry nowadays is that they love each other, and that certainly wouldn't apply.'

His face went rigid. 'Plenty of marriages are made for other reasons than love, and work well. I can offer you far more than the meretricious coin of sexuality with no ties, no deeper feelings. Sooner or later you're going to agree to marry me, because you want your children. I see the way you look at them when you think no one's watching—with hunger and pain.'

'I thought you had me tagged as a fair-weather mother,' she retorted acidly.

'I was angry,' he said. 'One look at your face when Rosie fell off her pony last night told me all I want to know about your feelings for them.'

'You might be content with a second-best marriage,' she snapped, driven almost to desperation by his un-hurried, relentless determination,'but I'm not. I won't live in Natalie's shadow all my life.'

Harshly he said, 'Natalie is dead.'

'No, she's not. Apart from your bed the house is exactly how she left it. Barbara refers to her in every second sentence. You look at the photo of her whenever you come into the morning-room. The children are en-couraged to talk about her all the time——'

'Stop right there,' he ground out. 'The children talk about her because she was their mother. She loved them and they loved her; I don't want them to forget her, ever.'

Perdita said unflinchingly, 'No one wants to forget her, Luke. I loved her, too. But it's inevitable that she should fade until she's a lovely memory in their minds. I don't see any signs of that happening. I'm not Natalie; I never will be. I can't replace her. Apart from anything else, I'd want to change things, and your reaction doesn't make me feel at all confident that I'd be able to.'

He said curtly. 'You can change whatever you like.'

'You don't understand. I am me, Luke, *myself*, not Natalie's shadow, not the empty vessel you used as breeding stock——' She stopped, appalled by the words that came tumbling from her lips.

His face froze into an expression of fury. Perdita's heart thudded into overdrive; for a fleeting moment sheer, unadulterated fear made her feel sick and shaken.

'You insinuated something like that before. What the hell do you mean by it?' he demanded.

She might as well get it out into the open; hidden, it was poisoning her.

Her eyes searched out the stark, chiselled features, the arrogance and anger stamped on his face. 'Isn't that what you did?' she challenged. 'Did you keep tabs on me, Luke, and decide that as I was so *conveniently* pregnant you might as well have your own children? Of course it would be a nuisance if I kept coming back to see them—they might not be so grateful, so much *yours* if they knew they had a birth mother not too far away! Somebody went to enormous lengths to lose files and hide information; somebody didn't want me ever to find out where my children had gone, or for those children to find me. Is that why the letters I wrote to Natalie after I went overseas weren't answered? Did Natalie ever get them, I wonder?'

'She got them.' His voice was soft, almost without expression, issuing between lips that barely moved. A muscle flicked in his jaw and as she watched his hands clenched into fists, lethal as his eyes, his voice.

Panic kicked nauseatingly in her stomach, but she refused to back down. 'I can understand why you wouldn't want me around—as you've already pointed out, it would be damned difficult to explain to them that you'd slept with your mother's seventeen-year-old cousin and got her pregnant. It would be much more convenient if you just made sure that I'd never be able to trace the twins. Unfortunately for you, there are always ways and means, and as you must know, if you've got the money to pay for it, information is usually procurable. The private detective I hired has built up contacts over the years, so he got a lot further than most. He told me that there were some interesting, unusual aspects of the children's adoption, but that so many files were simply not there, and those he found had such great chunks of information missing that it was impossible to prove anything illegal had happened.'

Luke asked silkily, 'Just what *are* you accusing me of, Perdita? Say it outright.'

'I'm not *accusing* you of anything,' she said, meeting his hooded arctic eyes with what she hoped he'd assume was equanimity. 'I just want to know the truth.'

Still in the same quiet voice he said, 'The *truth* is that we had put our name down for adoption a year before you sneaked into my bed that night. The *truth* is that I didn't know you were pregnant. Natalie and I were in America those May holidays, and in Australia in August, so I didn't have to tell her not to invite you up again because I never wanted to see you again. The *truth* is that in September we were asked whether we'd like twin girls, and although I had reservations Natalie fell in love with the idea. When she saw the children she fell in love with them.' His voice was low and deadly, filled with a flat contempt more searing than any overt signs of anger. 'How could I have known the children were yours?'

The colour the sun had kissed into her face died away, leaving her white and shaken, but she said through her teeth, 'I did not sneak into your bed that night!'

'Oh, of course, I'd forgotten! Natalie suggested you sleep there.' His tone told her what he thought of that.

She bit her lip. 'She did, but I can see I'm not going to convince you.'

'No,' he agreed cold-bloodedly, 'so you might as well stop trying.' He went on with a hard lack of compromise that grated, 'I'm not going to dignify any of your absurd accusations with a denial. If Natalie didn't answer your letters, it was because she thought it best not to. Perhaps she wasn't quite so unaware of what happened that night as we both hoped. And in answer to the tirade of a few minutes ago, yes, I loved Natalie. Death doesn't kill love, you know. But I'm not obsessively chained to her memory. Life goes on.'

It was the confirmation of all her fears. To the silent sound of her shattering heart she said quietly, 'I know. But you must see that it makes it impossible for me to even consider marrying you. There are too many unanswered questions.'

He looked at her with those astonishing, translucent eyes, green today as the shirt he was wearing, pitiless as Antarctic ice. In spite of his austere self-restraint, his compelling, potent magnetism made her catch her breath. It would be so easy to say yes—and she would spend the rest of her life wondering, watching, wracked by the pain of unsolved mysteries.

'And you don't trust me,' he observed ironically.

'Let's say I trust you about as much as you trust me.'

'Very well,' he said almost casually. 'Let's bargain. I won't ask you again, or make any reference to it, if you'll stay here until your wrist mends.'

She hesitated, looking down. The bandage showed clear and pristine against her white skin. A mirthless smile pulled at her mouth. 'I can't go anywhere, anyway,' she confessed. 'My wrist hurts whenever I try to put weight on it, so you're stuck with me until I can drive.'

'All right.' He turned his head to whistle up the dogs, and her heart turned over. How was it possible for her to love a man who didn't love her?

Only too easily.

He said evenly, as though nothing momentous had occurred—and for him, clearly it hadn't—'I'm going to check the fence over the hill. You can come if you like, but it will be muddy, and those boots don't look as though they'll cope with mud.'

'No, they were made for Italian streets,' she said, looking down at their elegance.

He nodded. 'It's pleasant here in the sun.'

Pulling her hat further over her nose—even in winter the sun had the power to burn her skin—Perdita let her breath out in a long, soundless sigh of relief as he strode up the hill with the confident, almost predatory gait she had remembered so many times over the years. The two dogs frisked at his heels, seeming to understand that today they were not expected to work.

Bess had wanted to go too, but had been sternly bidden to stay and guard, and with a Labrador's ineradicable sweetness of temperament was now sitting by Perdita, an expression of implacable resolve on her handsome face, obviously determined to defend Perdita to the death from any stray rabbit or little grey warbler.

Lord, Perdita thought, shaking now with reaction, that had been *stupid*. For a moment she had really thought Luke might hit her. Her accusations had sent him into a ferocious, dangerous anger that was only slightly less fearsome than his incredible control.

He said he didn't know she'd been pregnant, and she wanted so much to believe him. But someone had done their best to make sure she never found them.

According to Frank, the lost and mutilated files were the ones with the details of their parentage, and he was certain that the sabotage had been committed soon after they were born. Unusually for that time, Perdita had named Luke as the father. She could not bear the thought of her own children spending their lives wondering, as she had so often done, if one of the men they had passed that day in the street was their father.

Who else could it have been but Luke? He was the only person who stood to lose by that information. If Natalie had ever found out who the children's birth parents were, what would have happened to their fairy-tale marriage?

In fairness, she had to admit that there could have been other reasons for muddying the waters. Had Natalie's friend in the department pulled a few strings to help the Dennisons up the list, and then made sure no one would ever be able to find out what she had done?

Oh, yes, Perdita mocked, you'd love that to be the reason, wouldn't you? It would exonerate Luke.

Why couldn't she just accept that her children had been happy and dearly loved, and that she had found them again? Why couldn't she say yes, marry Luke, and settle down to be his wife and the girls' mother?

Because she wasn't prepared to be second-best. She had gained confidence in the last ten years, and she wanted more from life than to be a substitute mother, a substitute wife.

Luke's outburst had made it more than obvious that Natalie would always be first in his heart. If she married him she would have to live with that knowledge, and she didn't know whether she could.

Dragging in a deep breath of the clear, crisp air, she looked around. The Land Rover was parked in a small hollow so that no cool breeze chilled her skin, and she was becoming slightly too hot. After a moment she pulled off her windcheater, tossed it into the Land Rover and wandered across to lean on the fence. She closed her eyes and let the sweet, rich scent of bush and grass comfort her.

Although Luke owned Pukekukupa, the hill and a large acreage of bush had been vested in a reserve trust by Luke several years ago to ensure that no later Dennison could fell the immensely valuable timber. Over a hundred years before the forest had been saved from burning because even the land-taming pioneers could see that its ridges and deep gulleys running back up towards the bulk of the hill were too steep to farm.

It had been saved from logging because the hill was sacred to the Maori tribe in whose ever-fluctuating borders it stood, and because the first Dennison's adored wife had loved to gaze at its blue bulk from the nikau whare that was her home. She had managed to persuade her husband to leave it as it was, pristine, untouched; in fact, she had lived in that whare for an extra ten years rather than have the trees felled.

It was one of the few last stands of original forest left in the country, and many of the visitors who stayed at Pigeon Hill came to view it. Both station and reserve were bordered to the north by a road that served a couple of farms and acted as a fire access.

The frustrations and torments of the last months eased slowly away. Relaxed as never before, her body felt loose, gratified by an intense pleasure that extended outwards

from her bones as though every sinew and cell, every
nerve and tendon had been soothed and stimulated at
the same time.

She knew, of course, what had caused such physical
satisfaction. In spite of her dismissal of their union as
mere sex, last night had been a claiming, a soul-deep
surrender. Ten years ago she had been little more than
a child, and although Luke had made love to her with
heart-stopping expertise she hadn't been able to reach
fulfilment; during her affair with Howard she had been
shell-shocked, desperately searching for some sort of
meaning and commitment in her life.

Last night she had been a woman in Luke's arms, with
enough experience to understand what was happening
to her, a woman who accepted that nothing could come
of it, yet embraced the dangerous ecstasy and would
accept the consequences.

Their lovemaking had been fresh, new-minted, a pri-
meval union as old as mankind, as new as the tender
blades of grass pushing up beneath her feet. In her complete, unreserved capitulation there had been victory.

Straightening up Perdita walked away from the fence
and found a rock, sun warmed and smooth, poking
through the grass. Perhaps it had been ejected in the
fiery birth of Pukekukupa. She lowered herself on to it.
Bess padded over and collapsed faithfully across her feet,
closing her eyes.

'It's easy for you,' Perdita sighed, scratching behind
the soft ears. 'You can just give and give and give. I'm
not so courageous.'

The temptation to say yes was strong; her heart was
already lost to her, and even her treacherous mind urged
her to take that final step, subduing logic and common
sense with the glittering illusions of wishful thinking. It
was only her knowledge of herself, her intuitive under-
standing that for her and for Luke there would never be
any peace, any happiness if she married him without

being loved in return, that kept her from the alluring surrender.

Once you'd had a great love a practical marriage might seem sensible; for her it would be a living death.

Abruptly Bess sat up and whined, looking up the hill where Luke had disappeared.

Perdita said, 'Hush,' and lowered her head on to her knees, soaking up the immense silence punctuated only by the slow, exquisite chimes of tuis as they flew through the canopy in the bush. A native pigeon flew overhead, probably on its way to visit the guava bushes in the homestead garden, flying low enough for her to hear the sound of ripping silk it made as its big wings clove the air.

Perdita raised her head, narrowing her eyes against the sun to watch the bird out of sight.

Such a beautiful, trusting bird.

Bess suddenly sat up again, staring alertly into the depths of the bush. Once more she whined, something in her behaviour setting off alarm signals in Perdita's brain. Unable to stop herself, she looked around uneasily, the hairs on the back of her neck lifting.

But this was New Zealand, not New York. Danger couldn't sneak through these smiling paddocks and bush-clad hills.

At that moment a fusillade of barks erupted from over the hill. Startled, Perdita leapt to her feet as Bess joined in, her deep voice echoing over the trees. Suddenly through the cacophany came the sharp sound of a rifle shot.

'Luke!' Perdita whispered. He hadn't had a gun with him.

As though she had given permission, Bess took off up the hill, barking on a note far removed from her usual sound.

'Oh, my God!' Perdita stated after her, wondering what she should do. Her desperate gaze swung from the dog to the Land Rover with its cellphone. Although every instinct urged her up the hill to Luke, she raced across to the vehicle, snatched the cellphone up and dialled.

It took terrifying moments for her to get the operator, but at least she didn't seem to question Perdita's reasons for ringing. Almost immediately she was handed on to the police, who took the location and tried to convince her that she should stay by the Land Rover instead of going up the hill.

'No, I'm going,' she said firmly and hung up.

Barking from the dogs filled her ears as she ran up the hill, devoutly thankful that she was fit. Once she stumbled, landing heavily on her sprained wrist; pain shot up her arm but she staggered to her feet and pressed on. Some memory of cowboy films persuaded her to follow the cover of a clump of native bush to the brow of the hill. Afraid to look, she finally forced herself to peer through the screen of manuka branches.

Her heart jolted as she saw Luke. Moving with speed and an astonishing lack of noise, using every bit of cover, he was racing towards her. He didn't seem to be hurt. Dizzy with relief she dragged in a great, gulping breath. Somewhere in the reserve the dogs were barking ferociously; Perdita winced at the sound of another shot, watching with desperate eyes the man coming up a narrow declivity in the ground.

Just before he made the crest he looked up, and said in a voice that made her blood congeal, 'Get out of here!'

Obeying the savage directive, she raced back to the Land Rover; by the time he arrived she was scrambling into the vehicle. He jumped in, switched on the engine and put it into gear, and they hurtled off down the track towards the homestead.

'What happened?' she demanded.

In answer he tossed her the cellphone, gave her a number to ring, and planted his boot on the accelerator. Perdita swayed, but punched out the number.

A man answered. Luke snatched the phone from her hand and began to talk in staccato sentences. 'Joe, it's

Luke. Contact the police. Pigeon poachers armed with .22s are in the reserve, just through from the Lone Kauri. They fired a warning shot. No, of course it didn't.'

The man on the other end burst out in a chatter of questions.

'I'm perfectly all right,' Luke told him impatiently. 'I set the dogs on to them but they won't hold them. They must have come in along the fire access road. I've got to take Perdita back to the homestead. I'll see you at the eastern end of the road as soon as possible.'

He tossed the phone back to her. Grabbing it, she gabbled, 'What are you going to do? You're not going after them, surely?'

'Yes.'

Her mouth dropped open. The sound of those shots still reverberated in her heart. She pressed her shaking lips together until her voice was steady enough to ask, 'How? What will you do?'

He bared his teeth. 'I'll head off down to the access road, run their vehicle into the ditch and immobilise it, then wait for the armed offenders squad.'

'This is no time for macho games! They've got a gun,' she said furiously. 'They could kill you.'

'They weren't shooting to hit. There's a rifle in the back, but it won't come to that.' He paused, then said in what he probably thought was a conciliatory tone, 'Don't worry, I'm not going to do anything stupid.'

In a high-pitched, incredulous voice she declared, 'Going after them is stupid! How long will it take them to get down to their vehicle?'

'At least an hour. Plenty of time for me to drop you off at the homestead and get there.'

Perdita felt sick. She couldn't let him go down there by himself. She said tentatively, 'If you're sure we could get there well before them——'

'No.'

'But if there's no danger——?'

'No. You're not coming with me, and that's final.'

There was nothing but implacable determination in his voice. They were still heading at a frightening pace back to the homestead. She suggested urgently, 'You could put me out here and I'll walk back.'

'No.'

'Why?'

'The quickest way to get down to the road will be for them to come out into the paddocks and make a run for it. You'd be too close—they might think a hostage would be a good idea.'

Surrendering, she worried her lip with her teeth. 'I rang 111 when I heard that first shot,' she said.

He gave her a sharp look. 'Good girl. What did you say?'

When she told him, he nodded. 'Great, so the armed offenders squad will be on its way.'

'Where does it come from?'

'Whangarei.'

Outraged, terrified for his safety, she protested, 'That's at least an hour away! Luke, leave it to the police.'

'They are not getting away with it,' he said steadily. 'That land is mine, and I'm not letting any money-grubbing, dirty scum shoot every pigeon on Pukekukupa so that they can put money in their pockets to drink away.'

Knowing that she wasn't going to be able to dissuade him, she was silent for the rest of the way, staring sightlessly through the windscreen at the blue and green and gold day.

Back at the homestead, Luke stopped long enough to let her off and collect two more dogs, then swung away in a spurt of gravel, heading, she realised with dread in her heart, towards the north.

No one was in the house. She looked vaguely around, remembering that Barbara had intended to go into Manley to shop. The house was locked up.

On the chilly little terrace she sat down and said out loud, 'This is ridiculous!' trying to rid her brain of the hideous images that danced there. 'This whole garden needs a complete rearrangement so there are places to sit out of the wind!'

She even tried to work out what she'd do if it was hers, but after a moment she got up and walked restlessly around the house, rubbing arms that were suddenly gooseflesbed. Although the sun still poured benignly down she needed the windcheater she'd left in the Land Rover.

All she could think of was Luke in danger, threatened by men who hadn't hesitated to shoot at him. Inside she could hear the telephone ringing; she had taken her shoe off and was ready to break a window when it stopped suddenly.

An hour later the Land Rover came roaring up, followed by two other offroad vehicles. Luke swung out from behind the wheel, big and dangerous. Three ebullient dogs poured out behind him, joining the ones that leapt out of the other vehicles. She didn't recognise the other men, but assumed one was Joe.

Perdita ran towards Luke, her emotions naked, revealed in her face. 'Are you all right?' she demanded.

His eyes gleamed. 'I'm fine,' he said, and hugged her close to him.

A musky trace of excitement was mingled with his clean male scent. His strong arms were a haven, and for a moment she was still, almost fainting with relief. But she forced herself to draw back and demand, 'What happened? I've been frantic.'

'We got them,' he said.

'Thanks to you,' one of the men said on a dry note. 'Just don't ever do it again. Bloody near gave me a heart attack to come around that corner and see you holding them at bay.'

Perdita said, 'What?'

Luke shrugged. 'I immobilised their vehicle then waited for them.'

'Why?'

He looked at the man who had spoken, then said crisply, 'They shot Bess and Jock. They were laughing about it and firing at Sam.'

She felt his rage as though it was her own. 'I see,' she said, and indeed she did.

It didn't surprise her when he went back to the reserve after he'd made his statement to the police, and searched for the bodies of his dogs. Barbara had come home by then. She wanted to talk, but Perdita, too shocked to be able to do more than tell her the bare bones of what had happened, excused herself as soon as possible and went out to sit beside the swimming pool, as far away from the house as she could get. There, alone at last, she huddled her arms around her to shelter her from the chill that sprang from deep inside her.

Those hours of waiting had told her one thing. Life was not a given thing. Luke could have been shot that afternoon. He still didn't think the man had actually aimed at him, but nevertheless the bullet had come close.

He could, she thought, have been killed instead of Bess and Jock.

And she would have mourned him for the rest of her life.

Death was final. She had made up her mind not to marry him, but he would have been there, in her world. Now, shaken and shivering, she realised that second-best would be better than never seeing him again.

The sound of the Land Rover brought her head up. She walked swiftly to the garage, and saw with a jolt of pain that he had found the dogs.

His features were locked in an anger so intense he was unreachable. 'Jock's alive,' he told her. 'The bullet broke his leg, but he'll be all right.'

'Bess?'

At his curt shake of the head Perdita's eyes burned with unshed tears.

'Don't take it so much to heart,' he said almost gently. 'She died instantly, and she wasn't a young dog. This one will be fine once his leg's healed.'

Jock swiped his hand with a pink tongue. At the sight of Luke's lean fingers fondling the black ears, Perdita gulped.

Luke looked up and surveyed her face with unsettling thoroughness. 'You're as white as a sheet. Have you had any lunch? No? Get Barbara to make you some, and drink plenty of sweet tea with it. I'll take Jock into the vet and then get Bess buried before the girls come home.'

She said diffidently, 'Perhaps they'd like to conduct their own funeral service?'

'They've seen enough of funerals,' he said harshly.

But the girls came home before he did, and it was Perdita, afraid that they might learn of the dog's death in a manner that would hurt them, who told them about Bess.

Diving into her embrace, Rosie burst into sobs on her shoulder. The colour leached from Olivia's skin, but although her expression was agonised she didn't let the tears that collected in her eyes fall. When Perdita extended her free arm she came slowly across and allowed herself to be hugged.

'She died very bravely,' Perdita said, steadying her voice with an effort.

Rosie's sobs redoubled; Olivia turned into Perdita's other shoulder and wept without noise.

By the time Luke arrived back they were red-eyed but composed, although Rosie burst into tears again when he came in. Perdita had told them about the poachers, but hadn't mentioned the bullet that so nearly hit their father.

He was wonderfully tender with them both. However, there was nothing tender in the look he directed at Perdita when Rosie asked if they could bury Bess properly. Perdita shook her head, and gradually the icy fire in his gaze eased.

'If you want to,' he said, hiding his reluctance.

They buried her under an apple tree whose fruit she particularly liked, the girls saying an odd assortment of prayers in trembling voices. Perdita's eyes burned; if she could ensure it they would never suffer another pang of grief, she thought fiercely. But it was clear that this was cathartic for them, and by the time everyone, including Barbara, had sung 'All Things Bright and Beautiful,' Rosie was smiling, and even Olivia looked relaxed.

On their way back to the house she slipped her hand into her father's and asked softly, 'Can we have a puppy, Daddy?'

His eyes met Perdita's. His were cool and translucent; she knew that there was a hint of pleading in hers. Squeezing his daughter's small paw, he said, 'Yes, of course. But not just now, darling. We'll wait a little while.'

Lethargy overtook Perdita after dinner. All that adrenalin, she thought, with no place to go. She had to battle a tiredness that made her want to curl up and cry, and then hide away from the world until her heart had mended.

Instead she had to smile at her children as though they were no more than attractive strangers, and climb back into the glossy armour she had made so carefully for herself, armour Luke had smashed without even trying.

The following three days were oddly calm, the deceptive tranquillity of tension kept under tight control. During the long afternoon she'd spent waiting for Luke Perdita had made her decision; if he asked her again to marry him she would say yes.

For some reason she didn't want to explore, she didn't tell him. Instead, she enjoyed her daughters, discovering more about their likes and dislikes, oddly enough seeing some of herself in each, although Olivia was more like her than Rosalind, who, according to Luke, took after his mother's side of the family in both looks and personality.

They appeared to accept her without question; one afternoon when Juliette Robinson arrived, and stayed for an hour or so, Rosalind waited until she had gone before saying with a guileless satisfaction, 'This is what it used to be like when Mummy was here. People in all the time.'

'People still come,' Olivia pointed out with her typical concern for exactitude, although she smiled at Perdita as she said it.

Rosie wrinkled her nose at her. 'Don't tease. You know what I mean; ladies drinking tea and laughing and talking.'

Olivia smiled. 'Yes, I do,' she agreed. 'Perdita, did you know Mrs Robinson when you used to stay here?'

'Quite well. Once she tried to teach me how to ride.'

'What happened?'

'The horse pigjumped and I fell off.'

Olivia joined Rosie in a grin. 'Daddy should have taught you,' she said. 'He's really good. He doesn't shout at you when something goes wrong.'

'He did give me one lesson,' Perdita admitted, 'but I think he decided I was utterly hopeless, because he never offered again.'

Rosie said comfortingly, 'Never mind. Lots of people can't ride. You look beautiful.'

Perdita's heart swelled. She had to stop herself from dragging Rosie into her arms and holding her close. Rosie might be affectionate and sympathetic, but it was too early in their acquaintance for spontaneous hugs.

Perdita had missed so much, so much—all the childhood cuddles, all the funny little things of no importance, all the fun—and all the pain, too—of being a mother.

At least, she thought bracingly, the girls had been loved and cared for. Smiling at the earnest little face in front of her, she said, 'Beauty is as beauty does.'

'What does that mean?'

'Physical beauty is just an accident. The real test of beauty is character; what sort of person you are, the way you behave. That's the important thing, not how you look.'

Rosalind shook her head. 'Claudia Austen said you'd be stuck-up,' she said, 'but we told her you weren't, didn't we, Liv? I think you're very beautiful, and nice, too.'

Putting down her pen, Olivia regarded Perdita solemnly. 'Did you get too old to be a model? Claudia said you must be because otherwise why did you stop?'

Perdita said quietly, 'I got tired of spending half my life in jets.'

Olivia nodded, but Rosie said eagerly, 'I wouldn't! I want to see everything in the whole wide world!'

'If you want it badly enough, one day you'll probably do it,' Perdita said, loving her for her enthusiasm.

'What are you going to do now you're back in New Zealand?' Olivia asked.

'Yes, what *are* you going to do?' Unseen, Luke had come in.

Perdita directed a sharp, accusatory glance towards him, met bland eyes almost the same colour as his jersey. 'I'm not sure yet,' she said stiffly.

'But you're working on it?'

She nodded, looking away. The girls were watching, their eyes as alert as his.

'We'll be sorry to see you go, won't we?' he said, looking down at his daughters.

Olivia's glance travelled from her father's face to Perdita's set one; she nodded, but Rosie said, 'Oh, yes! Daddy, Mrs Robinson came today and she and Perdita sat and talked and laughed and it made me think of Mummy when her friends came!'

Something went rigid in Luke's expression. Touching Rosie's bright hair, he said gently, 'Perhaps I should invite lots of women in and talk and laugh with them.'

Rosie's green eyes crinkled. 'No, Daddy, they don't do that with you. They look at you with silly looks on their faces——'

She strutted away from him then turned, her mobile little face twisted into an expression in which it wasn't hard to see the slow, languishing glance of a violently attracted woman. Long lashes fluttered; she gave her startled father a soulful smile and let her small, brown hand rest lightly on his sleeve as she cooed, 'Oh, but Luke, darling——'

'That's enough,' Luke said, his expression—a mixture of shock and unwilling amusement—for once easy to read.

Rosie's gaze swung to Perdita. 'If you married Perdita,' Rosie continued offhandedly, 'you wouldn't have to bother with all those others. Olivia and me——'

'I,' Luke corrected automatically, his gaze very keen as he surveyed Perdita's still face.

'I talked about it, and we like her. She doesn't go all gooey and stupid when you come into a room, and it would be neat to have a mother we call by her proper name. Nobody else does at school. And she's famous.'

Perdita couldn't prevent her laughter pealing forth. After a surprised moment Luke joined her, leaving both girls looking from one to the other, Rosie a little affronted, Olivia as though something interesting had just been revealed to her.

'I'm flattered,' Perdita said quickly, before Luke could speak, 'but if that happened I'd be your stepmother. I might turn all crabby. Stepmothers can, I believe.'

'That's only in fairy-stories,' Rosie said bracingly. 'I know some stepmothers and they're nice. You'd be nice too.'

Perdita didn't have any answer to that. Without looking at the man who stood watching her, she said lightly, 'So are you, Rosie. Unfortunately, things aren't quite that simple.'

The two girls looked at each other and then at their father. Rosie said, 'But we thought——' She stopped, her troubled eyes going to Olivia as if seeking help.

'—that was why you were staying here,' her sister supplied. Eyes going from her father to Perdita, she hesitated, then finished, 'We both thought it would be a good idea.'

Luke said calmly, 'Well, now that Perdita and I know how you feel, we might think it over.'

To Perdita's shock, Rosie burst into noisy tears and ran out of the room. Scrambling to her feet, Olivia said intensely, 'I told her it might not be true, but she was sure it was,' and followed.

Perdita said, 'Should I go——?'

'No, I'll go up in a minute. Olivia will calm her down.'

Olivia, it seemed to Perdita, took rather too much responsibility for her more volatile sister's moods, but saying so wasn't going to help matters now. Rosie's artless remarks had precipitated a confrontation she had been trying to avoid. While she had waited for Luke, unsure whether he lived or died, it had seemed inevitable that she marry him.

But now that the exaltation of peril had passed, common sense had crept back with its caveats and questions, its infuriating logic.

She cast a fleeting look at Natalie's photograph, and felt the familiar pang of apprehension streak down her backbone. Marriage with Luke would give her so much—and take so much from her.

Outside the winter's quick dusk was coming down. Luke went across to the windows and pulled the curtains shutting out the bleakness.

He said evenly, 'I'll go and see to Rosie, and then I think we need to talk.'

CHAPTER SEVEN

QUICKLY restored to her usual sunny temperament, Rosie came down with her father after ten minutes or so, her face clear of tearstains.

Perdita had spent those minutes with Olivia. She enjoyed the older girl's quiet intelligence, the way she weighed things up. If she had been loved she might have grown up like Olivia, grave, thoughtful, but with the bone-deep confidence that only security gave. Olivia showed no sign of the hunger for affection that had driven the young Perdita.

After dinner they spent an evening playing a hilarious game of Scrabble, then another of poker, during which Olivia displayed a card-sharp's temperament and took her father down for an extra half-hour up on Saturday night.

Then it was time for bed. After a cheerful goodnight Perdita watched with sombre eyes as the three of them went out. Inevitably her gaze returned to Natalie's photograph.

How lovely she'd been! Famed for her charm, for her laughter and wit, for her generosity...

For the first time Perdita wondered just how much effort it had taken for Natalie to be the perfect wife, the perfect hostess, the perfect mother.

A chunk of wood clattered noisily in the hearth. She pushed the embers together, added another log, and was sitting back in the chair when Luke came in.

'All right?' she asked, looking up from the magazine she was pretending to read.

'Yes, they're fine.' He sat down, legs stretched out to the welcoming warmth of the fire. The strong muscles in his thighs flexed beneath the expensive trousers. Even for an evening at home with his children Luke wore well-tailored clothes. Against the pale walls his profile was a confident, disturbing line.

Disciplining her expression, Perdita said, 'If I do marry you, Luke, is it just for the children?' Her fingers came up to touch the gold locket for a second. 'Because if it is, I don't think I can do it. I'd rather leave Pigeon Hill and keep in touch with the children by letter.'

Eyes narrowed, predatory as an eagle at the still moment before the beginning of that fierce, lethal plunge towards ground, he asked, 'What made you change your mind?'

'About what?'

'About marrying me. The last time I asked you said no in no uncertain terms. Now it sounds as though you're considering it—if I can give you the proper reassurances.'

'I don't even know what the proper reassurances are,' she cried, rubbing a finger across the tense skin between her brows.

He hesitated. 'Have you ever wondered why we want each other so much?'

Shock robbed her of speech. Unable to look at him she swallowed, finally muttering, 'You ask some damn fool questions. That's not the issue.'

'It's part of it. I need to hear your answer.'

She could lie, but she had lied to him enough. Now she needed to be honest. 'Of course I have,' she said raggedly.

'So have I.'

Her heart began to pick up speed. Still keeping her face averted, she touched suddenly dry lips with the tip of her tongue.

'So?' she said nervously. 'Sex is fairly common currency, Luke.'

'Don't knock it,' he said, the words infused with irony. 'I want a wife,' he went on. 'I want companionship and laughter and, yes, sex. I'd like other children. And I need a wife who loves the girls. Shall we start again,

Perdita? This time with no hidden agenda, no feelings of remorse or anger or grief.'

'It's not that easy,' she said wistfully.

'Not even for the children?'

She watched her hands curl into fists. Could she marry him for the children? But it wouldn't be just for the children . . .

'It wouldn't work,' she said on a raw note of tension.

'Why not? We want each other, we both love the children, and they need a family.'

She said quietly, 'The afternoon you caught the poachers, I thought that if anything had gone wrong——'

'If I'd been killed, you mean? There was no possibility of that, but if I did die, you'd have no claim to the girls,' he said equally quietly. 'Not unless you married me.'

It took her a moment to realise the implications, but when she did she said urgently, 'No, no, that's not what I meant——'

He was smiling, the same humourless quirk that twisted his mouth when he listened to her deny creeping into his bed intent of seduction. 'No?'

Beneath her restless fingers the material of her trousers was smooth and satisfying. She realised she was running her hand up and down her thigh, and linked her hands together in her lap. Choosing her words carefully, she said, 'I gave the children up ten years ago. I have to live with that decision.'

'Why? To punish yourself?' His voice was scathing. 'I thought you were more mature than that, Perdita. The past reaches forward to colour the present. What happened ten years ago is still influencing us all.' His wide shoulders lifted. 'We don't have to worry about sexual compatability,' he said bluntly, 'so it's down to companionship. If you feel that you couldn't bear to live with me, then of course you must say so.'

He was so coldly pragmatic she was sorely tempted to throw his insulting proposal into his teeth. Then she saw the pulse beside his mouth; the tiny betrayal summoned a faint glow of hope.

She had steeled herself for renunciation, persuaded herself that it was the only thing to do, and now she was having to go once more over the same endlessly re-hashed arguments.

Could she bear to live with him? Over the years she had longed for him with a fervour that had made any other relationship impossible, and part of the reason she had come back was because she wanted to be free of that hangover.

Yet if there'd been any chance of that, surely the ten years in exile would have blunted the edge of her love?

He was offering a deadly blend of paradise and pain. If she married him there would be no going back; she would stay with him until the girls were off their hands. They had had enough grief and insecurity in their lives. And if there were other children...

'Is it such a difficult decision to make?' he asked, velvet-voiced, reaching out a hand to cup her cheek.

Sensation sizzled along her nerve-ends, setting fire to her body, tightening her breasts. She said thickly, 'Don't you dare use sex against me!'

His mouth twisted with its customary irony. 'I'll use anything I have to. If there were less riding on your de-cision I'd give you the opportunity to make it unclouded by passion. As it is...'

His final word was breathed against her lips. Angrily she blurted, 'No,' but she knew that for once the old cliché was right: whatever her lips were saying, she meant yes.

The flicker of triumph in his eyes betrayed him. It was that which gave her the strength to pull away.

'No,' she repeated sharply, 'this is too important. I need to think.'

'What good has thinking done?' His smile was self-derisory. 'You've spent the last three days trying to come to some decision, and you still haven't made up your mind. I've thought too, spent hours in the middle of the night trying to work out what to do, and got nowhere. All I know is that I can't forget the smooth welcome of your body, the fierce heat that surrounded me, the wild, consuming fire that ate through all the constraints I put on my behaviour, and I want to lose myself in you again and again and again...'

'Stop it, Luke!'

'All's fair,' he said, not completing the saying. 'If you were my wife, you could adopt the children, so that if anything did happen to me, they'd be safe.'

'Nothing's going to happen to you,' she said fiercely, realising what she had said too late to recall it.

His face was hard. 'Death has a habit of making its own agenda.'

With immense reluctance she asked, 'What will happen to them if—if I don't marry you?'

'I've appointed Natalie's mother to be their guardian, but she's too old to look after them full-time. They'd have to go to boarding school.'

She reacted to the conversational tone of his voice with fury. He was manipulating her, but even as the hot words surged forth he stopped them by saying, 'There's no one else.'

He was right. There were no other relatives. She said bitterly, 'You could change that to appoint me.'

'Marry me and I will.'

Frustratedly, her eyes glittering as they surveyed his uncompromising expression, she said, 'That's despicable.'

The stark, unhandsome face was unyielding, the pale eyes hard as the aquamarines they resembled. 'You can't have everything, Perdita. Both of us have to compromise. If you want the girls you take me with them.'

The prospect of life without him was bitter and desolate, with him, as his unloved wife, it offered heaven and hell mingled. All life is risk, she thought confusedly, but if I marry him I'll be risking so much—my heart, my happiness, my future...

'Is it so hard to make up your mind?' he asked, the slight, sensual roughness in his voice stirring secret tides deep inside her. 'I'll do my best to make you happy, Perdita.'

He would, she knew that, but could she risk her future on a second-best happiness? If she did, if she took that reckless step into an unknown future, the girls at least would be secure.

'All right, damn you,' she whispered, her heart shattering.

The girls were thrilled. Rosie greeted the news noisily and demonstratively, Olivia in a much more restrained manner, but both made their approval obvious. Of course that might have been because Perdita flew with them to Auckland to choose bridesmaids' dresses. Because he specialised in the elegant, richly restrained designs she favoured, she decided to use Clive, the designer Natalie had chosen to make the wardrobe she had given her those last holidays at Pigeon Hill.

He hadn't changed much in the intervening years. 'So you're back,' he said, eyeing the girls with faint alarm. 'Are you planning to work here, or is this just a flying visit?'

'I'm getting married,' she told him, her heart picking up speed as it always did when she thought of life with Luke, 'and these two are going to be my bridesmaids. So we want absolutely gorgeous dresses, and we want them in a fortnight.'

'Can't do it.'

She smiled. 'Yes, you can.'

He looked at her shrewdly, then transferred his glance to the two girls. 'We-ell, perhaps—who's doing the photos?'

'No publicity,' she said sternly. 'No leaks, no photos, no mention in the women's magazines. I want privacy and you don't need any more glitter on your reputation.'

Clive shrugged. 'Well, at least they're beyond the age of being sick with excitement. All right, for the most beautiful woman in the world, and her two lovely bridesmaids, I'll work miracles.'

Perdita enjoyed the discussions that followed. Not in the least intimidated, both girls had definite ideas; Rosie fell violently in love with ruffles and lace and one particular gold lamé, whereas Olivia evinced a quieter, but equally determined desire for plain fabrics and classical lines.

'She's got good taste,' Clive said as they drank coffee after the decisions had been made.

After one near quarrel and some very tactful guidance from Perdita, the twins had settled on a softly princess design in her favourite cerulean blue for Olivia, and a slightly more frivolous peach for her sister. As a sop to Rosie's desire for lace, Clive suggested petticoats to reveal just a hint of lace beneath the hem of each dress. Perdita chose the same lace to trim her dress of ivory silk.

Perdita picked up her coffee-cup, letting her gaze wander across to the girls who were enjoying themselves enormously with the assistant, trying on the exotic little clouds of tulle and feathers and costume jewellery that were newly fashionable for evening.

'Natalie's taste,' she said quietly.

'Ah, I wondered. There's a similarity in bone-structure, but of course you and she had a strong family resemblance.' He finished his coffee. 'Her death shattered me. She had great style; always charming, always fun, and with the kind of single-mindedness very few women have nowadays. When she bought clothes they had to be absolutely perfect, and I knew she'd show them off magnificently. None of this sloppiness that seems to be becoming more and more fashionable.'

Perdita hid a smile at the note of disgruntlement. Clive was growing older, and wasn't enjoying it. 'I don't know whether I've ever thanked you for putting in a kind word for me with Dorita,' she said, turning the conversation smoothly. 'Coincidence is a funny thing, isn't it. The job in her office was the first one I came across that I had any chance of getting, and when she asked me for a reference the only name I could think of was yours.'

He preened a little. 'Oh, well, it didn't cost me anything, and Dorita's not the only one who can spot potential! As soon as I saw you I knew you'd work well on the catwalk, you moved so beautifully, but I didn't know whether you'd photograph well, or had the guts or the stamina for modelling. Of course, the clothes Natalie bought for you persuaded Dorita into taking you on. She said as soon as she saw you in my clothes she knew you'd get there.' He sounded smug, as though he'd discovered her single-handed. 'If you'd turned up in a ghastly old T-shirt and jeans she might have turned you down, and then where would you have been?'

Perdita put down her coffee-cup with only the faintest tremor of her hand. Aloud she said, 'I have a lot to thank you both for.'

'Yep. A brilliant, meteoric career, for starters. Who's the lucky man?'

She knew it was useless to equivocate. With a warm, vague smile, she said, 'Luke Dennison.'

'Sensible of you, keeping it in the family,' he said irrepressibly.

It stabbed, but the expression on her face didn't alter. Getting to her feet, she said, 'We'd better go. We'll be back in a fortnight for fittings.'

Luke had come down with them on business, and they all had lunch together in a very upmarket restaurant in Parnell, Olivia and Rosalind refusing to tell him anything about their dresses because, as Rosie said importantly, 'It's a secret until the day, Daddy.'

Luke laughed and stopped asking, but afterwards, as they wandered around the aquarium beneath the Waterfront Drive, he looked at his daughters' fascinated faces and said, 'That was a good idea. Secrets bind people together.'

He was right, of course, although she hadn't sworn them to secrecy for that reason. Of course some secrets kept people apart. As they flew north over the long peninsula of Northland she looked down on hills and hollows already dim with dusk, and thought that in time she'd learn which was the stronger, that shared secret that had bound them together for the last ten years, or the others, the ones to which she'd never know the answers, the secrets that denied trust.

'You're very quiet,' Luke observed after dinner when the girls had finally given in to excitement and exhaustion and trailed off up to bed.

Avoiding his eyes, she nodded. They hadn't slept together since she'd agreed to marry him; he hadn't suggested it and although tension wound more and more tightly between them, and they had taken to speaking only of neutral subjects, she wasn't going to introduce the subject.

He said abruptly, 'After we're married you might like to redecorate the house. I know an excellent decorator if you need help. Tegan Sinclair has a very good name, and I think you'd like her.'

She nodded. 'The house does need refurbishing,' she admitted. And so did the garden, but perhaps she should show him she could be trusted with the house before suggesting she be let loose in the garden.

His eyes fell on the photograph of Natalie. 'You can get rid of that, too.'

Just as brusquely, Perdita said, 'Don't be an idiot.'

Was it thoughtfulness for her, or that he couldn't bear to see Natalie when he was putting another woman in her place? Except that Perdita knew she could never take her cousin's place.

'Thank you. The children would miss it.'

Later, sitting on her bed, she told herself sternly that she mustn't become paranoid about Natalie. It would be too easy to begin to resent her, simply because she had been loved by Luke and the girls.

Her mother would be caustically amused if she knew what she was thinking. Although more than willing to make use of Natalie, Katherine had been jealous of her, convinced that her charm was a cloak for a much less worthwhile character, and that she manipulated circumstances and people to suit herself.

'If my mother had taught me to pull strings as well as Aunt Marie taught her,' she'd said often enough, 'I'd have been able to persuade your father to stay with me. Instead I did the decent thing, and look where that got me.'

And if she continued to brood over things she couldn't change, Perdita decided as she turned impatiently over in her bed, she'd end up like her mother, embittered and unhappy, unable to accept that she was responsible for her own life.

She could feel sorry for her mother now. Everything Katherine had wanted had come to nothing. Abandoned with a child she couldn't love, Katherine had spent her life struggling with what must have seemed almost insurmountable problems. When Perdita had come back pregnant it must have been like the last straw.

Even when Perdita got the job in the modelling agency her mother hadn't been impressed. Astonished, actually, and almost angry, because the child she had valued so little had the promise of a future before her, Katherine had ridiculed her, making mordant, wounding comments, although she hadn't attempted to stop her.

The opportunity in Japan had swept Perdita unresisting to the other side of the equator; she could remember vividly the day she had been told that her mother had been so senselessly killed, and her mixture of emotions, regret, and grief, and a kind of bewilderment.

Perdita had flown back to a private funeral service where she was the only member of her family present. Although she had written to Natalie no answer arrived, although there were flowers from her cousin. That was when Perdita had given up hope, convinced that Luke had told his wife about their lovemaking. Natalie's defection had hurt almost more than her mother's death.

The funeral service had been bleakly impersonal. The minister didn't know the woman she was talking about, and there had been no friends; Katherine didn't make friends. The others mourners were made up of a couple of her mother's associates from work and a strange man who had left as soon as the service was over.

Packing up had been simple; Katherine had moved through the world without collecting anything beyond the bare essentials. A small box had held papers—Perdita's birth certificate, with its 'Unknown' in the place for the father's name, and a bundle of letters. Love-letters in an unknown hand. After looking for the signature and finding only a scrawled letter F, Perdita had burned them unread.

Lying in her bed now, her heart ached for her mother. She had so little to show for her life. It's not going to be like that for me, Perdita vowed. I'll love the girls and any other children we have, and although I'll never be as perfect a wife as Natalie, I'll love Luke just as much as she ever did. I'll make a life for myself, and when I die it won't be so—so bleakly.

Although the wedding was small, there were enough distant Dennison relatives and close friends of Luke to half fill the small, white-painted local church with its Victorian Gothic tower and windows. Natalie's mother was in England, so that was one hurdle Perdita didn't have to face. With any luck she'd have the time to become confident as Luke's wife before she had to deal with a possibly antagonistic cousin she had never met.

She had been slightly worried about Barbara Whittaker's reaction. However, after the first astonishment there had been nothing but co-operation.

'It's the perfect solution!' Barbara enthused, a comment that left Perdita feeling forlorn.

She might be going into this marriage for mainly practical reasons, and Luke certainly was, but it rubbed a raw patch in her soul when anyone else saw it that way.

Caterers did the reception; it had been informal and friendly, with the girls more the star of the show than she was. Perdita was devoutly thankful for that. Luke went through the motions without giving anything away. Outwardly, he was all that a bridegroom should be, his sophisticated urbanity only slightly tempered by the controlled fire at the back of his gaze whenever he looked at her, but she sensed a hidden distance in him, a detachment that cast a chill over her day.

And then everyone was gone, and the children were in bed, and she was alone with him. They had decided not to go away, although he'd suggested a couple of nights at one of the hotels in the Bay.

'I think the girls would be disappointed,' she had said without expression.

'Yes, I suppose they would. Ah well, we'll go to Fiji in the August holidays, perhaps.' He hadn't seemed to care.

Now, on their way up the stairs, she wondered desperately whether she had done the right thing. Ever since she had agreed to marry him she had watched him withdraw into the guarded citadel of his heart, impregnable, unreachable.

Well, it was done. She would just have to cope.

Perdita showered, and in the dressing-room between the bedroom and the room that had once been the larger bedroom of the suite and was now the sitting-room, changed into a nightgown she had bought on a masochistic impulse, a nightgown to wear for a lover, a pale, lovely champagne silk with shoestring shoulder straps and a skirt that fell on the bias from the neckline. The soft hue lent her skin some warmth and colour.

The sound of the shower being switched off hurried her into the bed. She pulled the covers up and lay looking around the room, mentally planning how to decorate it. A small gold cherub leered knowingly down from the sweep of white above the window. She hated it, hated this room, wondered why on earth she had ever been so silly as to think there might be a place for her at Pigeon Hill. She could, she thought stormily, strip the house of anything that reminded her of her cousin, but Natalie would always be ensconced there, the adored wife so cruelly snatched away, a beloved, tender memory for the children.

She was utterly, completely jealous of her, and it was time she admitted it.

Her first intimation of Luke's presence was the sudden darkness as the light went out. Then the side of the mattress dipped slightly. Perdita realised that she was holding her breath and let it go with a long noiseless sigh.

It was too late for second thoughts.

And why on earth was she acting like a shy virgin when only a few weeks ago they had made love? Ah, but then she had been swept off her feet; this wasn't wild, uncontrollable passion, this was the pragmatic legality of the marriage bed.

He might have been talking to one of the girls, or his dog, she thought hysterically, as he said, 'You're as stiff as a board. Are you exhausted? Come over here and I'll cuddle you to sleep.' Nothing but a mild concern echoed through his deep, textured voice.

Silently, wondering whether he wanted to make love as little as she did, she turned on to her side and put her head on his shoulder. His chest was rising and falling evenly, his skin warm and subtly scented against her nose, smooth and taut over muscles that spoke of hard work.

Perdita sighed again, and the coil of tension that had snarled up her reactions eased. Slowly, seduced by his unthreatening warmth, she relaxed.

'I don't think I told you how beautiful you looked today,' he said. His voice seemed to transfer directly from his chest to her ears, rumbling almost subliminally. 'I've never really believed in breathtaking beauty, but that's literally how you looked today. And thank you for making the day so wonderful for the girls.'

She yawned. Unconsciously her body curved against his, the whisper-thin silk flowing around him; the fragile material was no barrier to the heat of his skin.

'They looked stunning, didn't they?' she said huskily. 'And behaved beautifully. I'm glad they enjoyed themselves.'

'What was Juliette saying so earnestly to you just before you cut the cake?'

She hesitated. 'She thought this was a rattling good idea.'

'And do you?' His hand moved, tucking a strand of heavy amber hair behind her ear. Lean fingers traced the outer rim, sparking off a thin stab of sensation.

'Yes.' The word was barely audible. 'Yes,' she said a little louder, lifting a bonelessly lax hand to slide it across his broad chest.

And suddenly all her defences were stormed, as much from within as without. They made love with an abandon she couldn't restrain, didn't want to control, until exhaustion claimed them both.

For almost four weeks, while Luke and Perdita tried to sate themselves each night, the girls behaved as though they had never heard of wilfulness, or disobedience, or even misunderstandings.

Perdita knew it was too good to last, but when trouble blew up it came from a completely different direction from the one she'd expected. She had assumed that Olivia would precipitate the inevitable crisis, which just went to show, she realised afterwards, how little she understood these girls who were her daughters.

Because it was the openly affectionate Rosie, with her frequent demand for cuddles, her laughter and apparently complete acceptance of her new mother, who put an end to their small sojourn in paradise.

She wanted to stay with a friend, a new friend who had just arrived in the district. Sternly repressing the instinct to ask Olivia what she thought of this friend, Perdita said, 'No, darling, not until we know them.'

Her daughter's lip trembled. 'Just ring them up, Perdita, then you'll know them.'

'No, I need to meet them first.'

Rosie whined and pleaded, but didn't suggest they appeal to higher authority and ask her father, from which Perdita deduced that she knew Luke wouldn't allow it. It gave Perdita the confidence to continue refusing, pleasantly, but with determination.

Finally Rosie shouted angrily, 'You're not my real mother! You're not the boss in this house! I hate you! You're just——'

'That is enough,' Perdita said without raising her voice. Nothing, she hoped, showed of the sudden agitation that jagged tensely through her. 'Everyone loses their temper, but there's no need to shout and stamp and behave like a two-year-old in the throes of a tantrum. Go up to your room.'

Rosie began to sob noisily. Olivia's swift movement towards her was quelled by Perdita's glance.

'On your way,' Perdita said calmly. 'You can come down as soon as you feel better.'

She held her breath. This was the crunch; if Rosie defied her, she didn't know what she'd do.

Gustily tearful, her daughter stared at her for a few stretched seconds, before flinging herself around and racing from the room, effectively banishing Perdita's quick relief by lingering as long as she dared on the staircase, then wailing with studied dolefulness at the door of her bedroom. Should she tell her to go into her bedroom and close the door? Perdita dithered until Barbara appeared in the doorway.

'Everything all right?' the older woman asked tentatively.

Perdita said, 'Yes. Rosie's just getting over a fit of misery.'

The housekeeper opened her mouth, met Perdita's steady gaze, and closed it again. She nodded, and said calmly, 'I'm going home now. I'll see you tomorrow.'

Which Perdita construed to be a vote of confidence.

Olivia went on with her homework, a frown tugging at her brows as the sounds of Rosie's weeping echoed dramatically down the stairs. She had to be howling as loud as she could, Perdita thought, trying to ignore it. Little devil. But she found that her hands were shaking and a nasty hollowness in the pit of her stomach made her feel wretched and trembly.

Seeking comfort, she went outside. A southerly wind was buffeting the kauri on the ridges of Pukekukupa, and although none got to the garden, the air was chilly, faintly scented with the snowstorms battering the South Island a thousand miles away.

Gazing blindly at a magnificent magnolia in full pale pink glory, Perdita tried to forget that her daughter was sobbing her heart out. Had she been too hard? Would Luke back her up?

Irritated, she noticed that Brent Simons, who worked two days a week in the garden, was busy planting stocks in a bed in the middle of the lawn in a very municipal fashion.

Luke hadn't specifically referred to the garden when he'd suggested she might like to change things, but presumably he meant that as well as the house. For some reason she couldn't bring herself to start on the house; it seemed too much like a deliberate repudiation of the past, a blatant signal that the new broom was sweeping, perhaps a little jealously.

But the garden was different.

After greeting Brent she said, 'That ivy is making a mess of the summer house. I'd like you to pull it down and dig up the roots. A bougainvillaea would be nice there, or a skyflower.'

Brent looked at her. 'Mrs Dennison especially liked the ivy,' he said.

Although the words were delivered in a perfectly polite tone, it was clear that he would resist any suggestions she made for the garden.

The desire to bare her teeth at him and order him to do as he was told almost overmastered her, but of course she couldn't take her temper out on him. Returning his smile with one of her own, she asked without any inflection, 'When do you come next?'

'On Thursday.'

She nodded. 'We'll have it down then.'

'I'll have to ask Luke.'

'Of course.' She walked away, so angry that she could have hit him.

I'll go mad, she thought bleakly as she looked around the wide lawns. And then, No, damn it, I'm not a cypher in this place. I'll discuss the garden with Luke, and then Brent will do exactly what he's told to do or lose his job. It's time everyone learned that I am not Natalie, and I'm not going to live in her shadow any longer.

Racked with guilt for even thinking such heresy, she hurried back inside, to be greeted by an ominous silence oozing down from the top floor. Squashing her desire to tiptoe up the stairs and check to make sure that Rosie hadn't sobbed herself to sleep, Perdita borrowed a pencil and a couple of sheets of school paper from Olivia, still manfully doing her homework, and returned outside to measure and sketch and make notes.

Keeping in style with the house was all very well, Perdita decided militantly as she paced out the distance from the corner of the house to a huge magnolia tree, but in a climate and soil where growth tended to riot with an almost tropical fervour, Georgian symmetry needed some adjustment.

The terrace would look far more inviting if instead of the omnipresent ivy there were old-fashioned roses to climb over its pillars, or a petrea with its brilliantly violet flowers, or perhaps a pink mandevillea to tone in with the old bricks.

And the swimming-pool was in quite the wrong place, a long way from the house behind high, clipped hedges where the sun only found its way in the height of summer.

She strode around to the back of the house, surveying the wide expanse of gravel there with a jaundiced eye. There was a perfectly adequate parking area at the front, so most of this could be converted into a terrace. It would be ideal for a big entertaining area with a pool that caught the sun. Setting her jaw she paced out more measurements and jotted them down until driven inside by a skiff of rain.

Olivia was waiting for her when she came back inside, her expression serious, her eyes cool. 'Rosie's feeling sick,' she said accusingly.

Hardening her heart, Perdita lifted her brows. 'Too much crying, I expect. That's how I feel when I cry for ages. Gives me a shocking headache, as well.'

Olivia nodded. 'Me, too.' Recalling herself, she went on, 'She wants to say she's sorry.'

'Nothing is stopping her.'

Olivia hesitated. 'Can she come down, then?'

Perdita said firmly, 'She must be the one to decide, not you. When she's ready to come down, she can.'

'I said I'd ask you——'

'Nobody has to ask me. Rosie must decide for herself when she feels better, not send you down as an emissary.'

Olivia frowned. 'But that's what it's like to be twins,' she explained.

Shaking her head, Perdita said, 'Rosie is the one with the problem, not you. Come on, now that the shower's stopped we'll pick some flowers to put beside your mother's photograph. Those camellias are looking a bit depressed, and yesterday when I was walking around the garden I saw that the violets are flowering.'

After a moment's indecision Olivia agreed. 'They were Mummy's favourite flower,' she said wistfully.

'I know. Once I carried a root of a special one all the way up in the bus from Auckland for her; it grew in the garden of an old lady next door to us, and when I told her that my best friend loved them, she gave me a piece of it.'

Olivia looked up. 'Why was Mummy your best friend when she was older than you?'

'Oh, we had a lot in common, your mother and I.' We both loved your father for a start, she thought ironically. 'How many violets do you think we can pick?'

They picked a big, fat fistful of them. Olivia was arranging them in a cut crystal vase beside Natalie's portrait when Rosie asked from the doorway, 'Where have you been?' Her voice quavered.

'Picking flowers,' Perdita said evenly. 'If you're ready to give up on your tantrum you can come in and help.'

There was a pregnant silence. 'A couple of sprigs of breath of heaven would set them off perfectly,' Perdita said conversationally. 'Do you know what breath of heaven is, Olivia?'

'Yes, I do.' After a troubled look Olivia left the room.

Rosie hovered in the doorway for a few seconds before finally coming into the room. Her bottom lip still jutted, and she was tearstained and mutinous, but without her sister there she was able to say, 'I want to come out.'

'Certainly.' Perdita smiled at her. She wanted to cuddle her until the tears had dried and the usual sunny smile was back, but instinct warned her not to. 'You only ever have to stay in your room until you feel like being better, you know. No one is forcing you to stay there.'

'Olivia told you——'

Perdita interpolated, 'I know you're twins, but Olivia is definitely not you, and not a messenger, either. You are the one who has to make the decision.'

Rosie didn't like that, but as Olivia had arrived back with three tiny sprigs of breath of heaven wafting out their spicy fragrance, she decided to ignore it.

When the girls were safely tucked up in bed and asleep, Luke looked up from the sofa where he was reading a farming magazine and said, 'Rosie seemed a little aloof.'

'She'll get over it,' Perdita filled in the last clue of the cryptic crossword and folded up the newspaper. She explained what had happened, although not Rosie's angry outburst. 'She's still cross with me for making her decide when she was to come out of her room, instead of accepting the overtures of peace she made through Olivia.'

He nodded. 'I wondered whether you had noticed. Rosie relies on Olivia to get her through unpleasant situations. Natalie said——' He stopped abruptly.

Perdita fixed him with a long look. 'Luke, I'm not going to fall apart if you say her name, or refer to her. It is, after all, her house I'm living in, her children I'm doing my best to be a mother to.'

Her husband I'm sleeping with, her life I've moved into.

The unspoken words burned on her tongue, were carved deep into her brain.

'All right,' he said after a taut moment, his lashes hiding his thoughts. 'Is that a hint that you want to make some alterations? Go ahead; I told you you could do what you like with the place.'

That hadn't been what she meant, but it was too good an opening to miss. 'I'd like to meet Ms Sinclair and talk about the house. The garden needs rethinking, too,' she said cautiously. 'The ivy should come down from the little summer house. It's awfully gloomy, and not good for the wood. A bougainvillaea would be ideal. Not the old-fashioned magenta one; there's a very pretty cream and buff and rose one that would look lovely there.'

'Plant whatever you like. I'd rather you consulted me before you take a chainsaw to any of the trees——'

'I wouldn't dream of touching the trees,' she said, scandalised until she saw the slight curve of his mouth. Such a small thing, yet it set her heart singing. Smiling back, she said, 'I'm quite good with a chainsaw, as it happens, but it's that wretched ivy I'd like to take it to. From Brent's response when I suggested it, I gather he thinks the garden is perfect and any changes would be sacrilege.' She spoke with a slight dry emphasis that didn't escape his notice.

Luke looked directly at her. 'I didn't know you were interested in gardens, or gardening.' His eyes drifted down to her hands, the long, elegant fingers neatly disposed in her lap, oval nails polished.

'Don't stereotype me,' she said lightly, irritation and disappointment lending enough of a bite to her tone to draw his brows together. 'I've always been fascinated by them. While I was modelling I studied landscaping and art as best I could.'

'I see. Do you have any other plans for the garden?'

She looked at him, wondering whether he was really interested. Probably not, but he was trying. Like her.

'Lots,' she said promptly. 'I'd like to convert that unnecessarily big parking area off the morning-room and kitchen into a terrace. It gets all the sun. A swimming-pool would be nice there.'

'We already have a swimming-pool,' he pointed out, adding laconically, 'which nobody uses.'

She nodded. 'Because it's inconveniently far from the house and too shaded by the trees. I'd like to change it to an ornamental pool. Look...' She pulled out the sketches she had made that afternoon.

Although his expression revealed nothing, he looked them over carefully. At last he said, 'This looks professional.'

'I told you I studied it.'

'All right, how would you set about it? I'd rather you had someone to help, someone with connections and contacts.'

She didn't blame him. Pretty sketches were one thing; to have the knowledge and stamina to see them through to fruition was quite another.

'And if Brent is being possessive,' he added with more than a hint of steel in his tone, 'remind him who owns the place.'

She nodded. 'It would cost a packet.'

His brows shot up. 'You're married to a reasonably rich man,' he said satirically.

'That's something we haven't discussed.' Putting the sketches down, she looked steadily at him, noting with a pang that he looked tired. The lines at the corners of his eyes were a little more deeply engraved, and the stark cheekbones seemed more fiercely sculptured than before. But then, she was tired, too. At night they made love with such passionate intensity that it was a wonder either of them could get up in the morning.

Conscious of colour stealing up from her throat she said hastily, 'Money. You are married to a reasonably rich woman.'

'I don't need your money,' he returned, his voice unyielding.

'I don't need yours, either,' she said stiffly. 'That wasn't what I meant. How are we going to organise our finances?'

'However you like. I would rather you didn't buy the girls too many presents, but apart from that it's yours, you do what you like with it. I'll continue to pay the expenses, and I will, of course, make you an allowance.'

Perdita's skin stung as though he had slapped her in the face. He couldn't have made more insultingly plain his determination to keep their lives separate.

Except in one place. In bed he didn't even try.

Very well, then, if the bed was to be the only place where they met as equals, she would make it so appealing that he would never want to stray from it.

The next couple of months went comparatively smoothly. Having tested the waters the girls relapsed into normal behaviour for ten-year-olds—basically good, with flashes of temper and defiance from Rosie, but nothing Perdita couldn't handle. Olivia began to relax in her presence, occasionally displaying a reassuring naughtiness. Perdita felt that she was no longer an abstract figure representing 'mother' to her daughters, but a real mother.

Her first dinner party was an ordeal, but it went off satisfactorily, and soon the district gathered her into its social life and she began to recognise people in the street.

In Whangarei she found a landscape gardener whose ideas fitted in with hers, a middle-aged woman who supplied the practical knowledge that Perdita didn't yet have. Slowly, messily, excitingly, the garden was transformed into something like her vision of it. The sea of gravel at the back of the house was transformed into a wide, brick-paved terrace that provided a wind-free sitting-out place while echoing in an informal manner the precision of the Georgian style; within a year plants would soften the starkness of trellis and pergola, tying the new area to both house and garden.

After some initial resistance Brent gave up being obstructive, just as Barbara gradually allowed her to do some housework. The workers on Pigeon Hill became people to her, not just names and faces, and she discovered in herself a sense of place; all her life she had been lost, and now she had found a haven for her soul.

In fact, the only person who showed no signs of accepting her was the one she most desperately wanted to. Her husband was courteous, thoughtful, exciting; he discussed things with her as though she was a real human being instead of the most beautiful woman in the world. At night they came together in incandescent passion that left them both hungry for more. Yet as the days and weeks and months took them through a wet spring and towards Northland's long, hot summer, she realised that she was eating her heart out for some sign of love, of affection.

Although she had gained so much, the glittering prize that was love hovered as tantalisingly out of reach as it had ever been. Risking everything, she had failed.

And she was going to have to live with that for the rest of her life.

However, there were always the humdrum chores of daily life to take her mind off the one thing she couldn't have, Luke's love. Picking up an armful of clothes from the laundry, she took them up the stairs.

As always there was a stray sock. Did they eat each other? she wondered, glowering at it. The attack of the cannibal socks. Perhaps he'd left one in his shoe. She looked in his wardrobe, eyeing the neat row of shoes. A hint of colour caught her eye. Bending down, she discerned a photograph album thrust almost out of sight to one side.

It didn't occur to her to leave it there. It was tucked so far to the back that if she thought at all about it, she'd have assumed it had been lost.

She picked it up, blew a little dust from the cover, and opened it.

A photograph of Natalie and Luke was the first thing she saw. She knew it; it had been taken on their honeymoon in Sydney by a street photographer. They were sitting at an outdoor café, Natalie's gamine-cut hair blonde and sleek and saucy around her face; Luke appeared infinitely younger, the controlled authority already there, but somehow less forbidding. This man didn't look invulnerable, Perdita thought. He was gazing at Natalie as though her person held all the world offered.

Perdita snapped the album shut so firmly that something stuck inside the pages was expelled by the sudden pressure of air.

A letter.

No, she thought, I'm *not* going to read this. She tried to poke it back, but it resisted. When she opened the pages a little way so that it would slide in easily, she saw with incredulous dismay that her name was written on the outside in Natalie's bold hand.

Shaking, she closed her eyes. Red spots danced beneath her eyelids as she slowly, carefully opened the thick, smooth paper of the envelope.

CHAPTER EIGHT

'DEAR Perdita,' she read.

Last night I saw you come back to Pigeon Hill, and
although it was only a dream the memory won't go
away. I think it must be an omen, and if it is, and you
do come back, there are a few things you should know.
By the time you read this I'll be dead. You can't know
how angry and bitter I feel about it. Life hasn't been
fair to me. I should have been able to have children,
sons and daughters for Luke, children who were truly
mine. Instead, I had to rely on you. Have you ever
wondered why I suggested you sleep in our bed that
night?

Perdita's heart throbbed heavily in her chest. The
words danced before her eyes, tilting drunkenly to one
side of the paper as her fist clenched. More than anything she wanted to throw the letter into a fire without
reading another word, but she knew she couldn't. Taking
a deep breath, forcing herself to ignore the sick chill in
her stomach, she read on.

We set you up, Luke and I. I made sure you'd be in
our bed, and he pretended not to know. I knew you
were fertile—remember we'd had that discussion about
the rhythm method a couple of weeks before, and we'd
taken our temperatures to see whether it actually
worked? I set that up, too. You always were grateful
for any help I could give you in that area of life.
Katherine should never have had you—she was totally
useless as a mother. But then, she didn't really want
you—you were her way of punishing everyone, including herself.

Luke didn't want to sleep with you, but he did it for me because we knew by then that I was barren. It was so utterly unfair; I'd made the perfect life for us, and then it all fell down.

Perdita stood abruptly, and the world whirled around her head. After a moment her sight cleared enough for her to read on.

Luke suggested we adopt, but I didn't really want anyone else's children in my life. Breeding is so important, I've always felt. He didn't really want it, either. He wanted his own children. Then I realised why you had been sent to me. You were family, and you were loving and sweet and nice—everything I wanted my children to be. So I made plans, and I wasn't really surprised when they worked. If it hadn't been for me the girls would never have been conceived, never been born. I gave them life, and no one could love them more.

It would probably bore you if I told you just how I manipulated things so that I finally adopted the twins. Even Luke doesn't know how I did it. I did nothing illegal, but I'm very good at planning, and I called on every contact I had. But I think it would have happened anyway—it was meant to be. When we brought them home I fell in love with them. No one tells you that you fall in love with babies. It was a pity I had to cut off contact with you, but there was no way around it; we could have coped if you'd just had one child, but you'd have realised that the twin daughters you gave birth to and the twin girls we'd adopted were the same, and that would have caused an awful lot of heartache to us all.

So I had to make sure you never came back to Pigeon Hill. I must say, I never expected you to turn yourself into a model. It was quite a shock when I started to see you in all the magazines; not the gangly girl I knew so well, but a tall, exquisite creature with a thousand looks and all of them seductive. And it was obvious you were having a whale of a time. I was almost envious sometimes. I hope you're just a tiny bit grateful, Perdita, because if it hadn't been for me you wouldn't have known how to behave, would you? You were such a little pagan when you first came up— sometimes I wondered whether I was ever going to be able to make anything of you. But I did; I created you, just as I created the girls. In every way that matters they are my children.

I taught them their manners, I loved them and looked after them; I was the one who adopted them when their real mother gave them away. The word 'mother' is going to mean me. I couldn't resist giving them Shakespearian names, although Luke didn't want me to do it—I suppose he thought you might guess, but I knew that wouldn't happen. Everything worked out so well it was obvious the gods were on my side. Until now.

Luke will marry you, because that will ease his conscience. I feel quite happy about that; it's almost like a pattern fate has woven around us.

You'll be happy, too. Not as happy as we were, though. We had something completely out of the ordinary, Luke and I, but he always liked you. And he enjoyed sleeping with you; I got him to admit that. Men, of course, are not as fastidious as women, and I suppose there's something rather primitively satisfying to the male ego in initiating a virgin. On my good days I hope you'll never understand just how painful that thought has been for me; when I'm feeling bad I find myself hoping you do.

Take good care of them, Perdita, or I'll come back and haunt you.

Perdita stared at the paper as though it was bewitched. Her eyes travelled past it to the photograph of Natalie and Luke, so golden together, so happy, so suited in every way.

'I don't believe it,' she whispered to the silent room, to a woman who had been dead for almost two years. But she did believe it. How often had she heard Natalie say that perfection was attainable—it just took hard work? She hadn't mentioned that it also needed the ability to manipulate others and convince yourself that it was *meant*!

Betrayal tasted bitter in Perdita's mouth, in her heart.

It was like removing a mask from a beloved face, expecting beauty and finding foulness beneath.

Natalie had used her. The guilt and pain of the last ten years meant nothing, were just so much futile, unproductive emotion. How ironic! She had been arrogantly sorry for her mother for looking backwards, wasting her life, and yet she had done exactly the same thing.

Natalie had manipulated her into Luke's bed, into his arms, and callously stolen the fruits of that cold-blooded coupling. In that first, intense revulsion, Perdita could have killed her.

'How dare you?' she whispered savagely. 'How dare you play God with my life?'

Sickened, shattered, she looked down at the photograph again. How could she ever have thought that she could love Luke? Forgiveness of such a cynical betrayal was impossible, yet she would have to endure it, because she couldn't walk out on the girls.

They were beginning to rely on her; some day they would love her, and that was more than she had aspired to for the past ten years.

So although she wanted to kill Luke, fling his perfidy in his face and make him *squirm*, shout and rage and smash things and teach him that he couldn't play dice with her heart and body without paying for it, she wouldn't. She'd lock her heart away. Plenty of women had lived in reasonable tranquillity with men who didn't love them, whom they didn't love. From now on she would expect nothing—*nothing*—from him, and eventually perhaps, when the first keen edge of anger and betrayal had died down, she might aspire to steady, somewhat humdrum contentment.

It sounded like a death warrant.

You should have known better than to read a hidden letter, she told herself wearily, even one with your name on it. Remember Bluebeard's wife.

A movement at the door jerked her attention away from the pages. Luke strode into the room; she saw the moment he realised whose writing was on the paper. He stopped. Shock loosened the constraints of his will; almost immediately, however, he reimposed control and all expression was wiped from the angular features, leaving only the splintered intensity of his eyes.

'Where did you get that?' he asked harshly.

Perdita found herself shaking with rage. 'In a photograph album in your wardrobe,' she retorted. 'Don't worry, it's addressed to me. How you must have laughed, both of you!'

He didn't move. 'What are you talking about?'

'This.' She flourished it, her mouth turning downwards into a sneer. 'Natalie wrote it to me when she realised she was dying. Apparently she thought I might come looking for the girls.'

He went white around the mouth, staring at her with flat, lethal eyes. 'What's in it?'

That involuntary physical reaction was confirmation enough.

'A confession, of sorts,' she said, feral rage building within her. 'Not that she believed she had anything to confess; apparently she just felt I should know how you and she used me to get your family.'

'Used?'

'As in manipulated, exploited, tricked, outsmarted! You used me,' she flung at him, the words sharp and hard as spears, 'for breeding stock, you and Natalie. Just as you're using me now as a mother and a wife.'

Something ugly glittered beneath his lashes. 'Indeed? I'm afraid you're going to have to explain what you mean.'

'It's no use lying—she's completely frank.' She didn't even attempt to hide the contempt and disgust in her words.

'Give that to me.'

Perdita bit her lip, but he said in a voice so empty of emotion that the menace showed stark and savage, 'You've gone too far to back out now. Show me this bloody letter.'

The heavy weight of her hair brushed against her cheek. He said her name in a kind of a soft snarl, and any opportunity for choice was past. Drawing a painful breath, she held the letter out.

Against the thick, white paper his tanned fingers made a shockingly primitive contrast. He didn't look at the letter. No hint of feeling escaped those autocratically sculptured features, the cruel, beautiful mouth, the narrowed intensity of his eyes, yet she could feel the force of his emotions like a vortex, fierce, irresistible.

Perdita walked across to the bed and sat down on the side. Exhaustion seeped through her in an obscene tide that robbed her bones of strength, her mind of anything but a primitive will to survive.

The soft crackle of paper as he opened the letter hurt her eardrums. She couldn't look at him, couldn't do anything but stare at the fat cupid that sat smugly in the drapes across the window. Tomorrow she'd ring the decorator, and the first thing to go would be that bloody cupid.

It was a symbol of all that she was never going to have, and by the time she had finished with this room it would be rich yet dramatically austere, relying on smoky colours and fabulous textures for effect, with not a hint of gauze or lace. Natalie, she thought viciously, would never recognise it.

The sound of Luke's curse jagged across her raw nerves with unexpected abrasion. Breathing deeply, she willed the linked hands in her lap to lie still and calm.

'And you believe this?' he asked in a voice that set every cell in her body leaping into terrified life.

'Why should she lie?' she asked monotonously. 'She was going to die. One usually tells the truth in such circumstances, I believe.'

'And if I tell you this letter is the fantasy of a sick brain, who will you believe then?'

Dragging her gaze away from the self-satisfied smirk of the cupid she concentrated on the bunch of jonquils, cool, deliciously scented little stars, on top of the bookcase. 'What difference does it make? I know why you married me. In that, at least, you were honest.'

Silence hummed between them, vibrant with unspoken emotions.

'You believe her,' he said quietly. 'You actually believe that I wanted children so much that I would seduce a girl, my wife's young cousin, in my care, in my house, to get her pregnant.'

She turned her head. He wasn't looking at her; his eyes were on the folded papers in his hand. His profile was outlined arrogantly against the pale wall.

'I've always known that you loved her enough to do anything for her.'

'Thanks for the vote of confidence in my integrity,' he said silkily. 'Obviously you have no idea how bloody insulting that is. I did not know you were asleep in my bed that night. I thought you were Natalie.'

Achingly, because she wanted so much to believe him, she said, 'Don't lie to me, Luke. I can take almost anything but lies.'

'Yet you'll believe Natalie's,' he said stonily. 'Even though, according to this, she lied to you and used you, you'd rather believe her lies than my truth. All right, let me tell you exactly what was going on that last summer. For a couple of years I'd been worried about her mental equilibrium. She longed to get pregnant, so much so that she'd got to the stage of only wanting to make love when she was likely to conceive. She seemed to think that she wasn't a proper woman, that her life was worthless, simply because she couldn't have three or four children. I was content to adopt, but Natalie didn't accept failure. It preyed on her mind. Even so, she wouldn't have taken such a long chance, with so little possibility of success.'

He walked across to the window and stood looking out at his domain, the great bulk of Pigeon Hill on one side, the garden and the trees, the green paddocks, the quiet cattle and sheep. His voice was strained, almost raw in the quiet room. 'Can't you see, Perdita, that this is a desperate attempt to claim some sort of responsibility for the twins' birth? She wanted so much to have children, she somehow managed to convince herself they were hers. And she wanted to convince you, by saying that she had planned everything.'

Of course that exonerated him completely. To Perdita, Natalie's assertion had the ring of truth.

'Yet she did discuss the fertile period in a woman's cycle with me,' she said remorselessly. 'I remember it very clearly—and that she brought the subject up. As for planning it—that was easy enough. You'd spent two days in Wellington, remember? Natalie simply went off to the Gardiners' without contacting your hotel, leaving me nicely parcelled like bait for a tiger in your bed. She even suggested the sleeping pill. In case I was restless, she said. I was, so I took it. Of course I didn't hear you come in, and I didn't realise you were in bed with me straight away, but——' She stopped, colour licking up through her skin in an apricot flood.

'But what?'

'I knew who you were almost immediately,' she finished beneath her breath. 'But it honestly seemed like another of my fantasies. I had a crush on you, as you must have known. I imagine I was painfully transparent.'

He said almost absently, 'I arrived home late, had a glass of wine while I read the paper, and then came up to bed.' He made a swift, angry gesture, looking at her with such bleakness that she recoiled. 'I should have stopped when I realised who you were. But I didn't. I couldn't. Because I wasn't immune to your shy, uncomplicated freshness. Yes, I knew you were in the throes of a crush. What I couldn't cope with was the fact that I wanted you, too.'

His fist clenched. 'And afterwards I was so sickened by what I'd done, so furious with myself for wanting you, and taking you, being unfaithful to Natalie, that I lost my temper.'

'I thought you lost it because you believed I'd seduced you,' she said woodenly. His cruel words and outright, instant rejection had haunted her for years. Still haunted her.

'That, too. You can't prove you didn't, can you, any more than I can prove I didn't know who you were that night.'

'She says in here——'

'If I say she's lying, who are you going to believe, Perdita?'

He sounded calm, but she could see the tiny muscle jumping in his jaw, and the pale eyes were compelling and intense.

She said roughly, achingly, 'I *have* to believe her. How did she know about my pregnancy? My mother didn't tell her. How did she know we'd slept together? Did you tell her how much fun it was to initiate a virgin?'

His hand crushed the letter. That white line around his mouth intensified. 'No,' he said, his voice a low growl of fury. 'I did not! But surely—even for Natalie—the odds of pulling it off, of a pregnancy, were too great!'

'What did she have to lose? Merely a night in your bed, and if, as you say, she wasn't interested in making love unless it was her fertile time, I don't suppose she counted that much loss.' She wanted to hurt him, wanted him to suffer just some tiny part of the anger and pain that were raging inside her.

His mouth twisted. 'No, she wouldn't have thought that much loss. All right, say she did plan it. She still lied when she said I had anything to do with it, or that I discussed that night with her. She made her plans without consulting me because she knew I'd have had nothing to do with such a heartless scheme.'

Perdita bowed her head. 'How do I know that?'

'Because eventually you're going to know me,' he said with disturbing authority. 'Well, enough to know that the whole letter is a farrago of lies.'

'Do you believe that she planned that night?'

He hesitated, his expression dark and withdrawn. Dreading his answer, Perdita scrutinised the chiselled angles of his face.

Finally he said almost indifferently, 'Yes, I think she probably did.'

Perdita said woodenly, 'So do I.' Her memories shattered, crumbled into dust, into lies and shams and masks, into trash.

He asked quietly, 'Do you believe that I had anything to do with it?'

She couldn't answer. Her longing to believe in his innocence overcame the hidden realist who taunted her with the knowledge that he had loved Natalie enough to see his children as the only way to save her sanity.

'I can't force you to,' he said, still in that same detached tone. 'But if you read the letter, you'll see that although she says we made the plans, all the way through she says "I did this, I did that," with no mention of me.'

Some unusual quality in his voice caught her attention, dragging it away from the turmoil inside her. She saw a face kept immobile by such merciless self-control that it resembled a mask. Perdita understood his need to convince her; the future of their marriage depended on it. It would, the relentless cynic inside her pointed out, be much more pleasant for him if he had a wife who didn't believe he had conspired to seduce her and get her pregnant, then take her children from her illegally.

She could ask to read the letter again, but if she did, instinct warned her, something irretrievable would be gone from their marriage.

And ultimately, as he had pointed out, it came down to trust.

All she had to ask herself was whether Luke would seduce his wife's young cousin who was living in his house, under his protection, for the sole purpose of getting her pregnant with his child so that he could adopt it.

And the answer was clear. Of course he wasn't. The Luke she knew was strongly moral, with high principles. He was no snob, dominated by the desire to have only his own blood at Pigeon Hill. There was no taint of the obsessive about him. Whatever her reasons, and Perdita thought she was beginning to understand them, Natalie had lied.

She said quietly, 'No, you wouldn't do that.'

He said even more quietly, 'You don't know how much that means to me.'

She risked a swift glance at him. He still looked the same, a hard, unhandsome man with an awesome impression of force and power. He would never be anything else, yet when they made love that tough, heavily muscled strength was tempered. He lost himself entirely in passion, but he had never hurt her; she had never even considered that he might. She trusted him utterly.

Now, she thought suddenly, now was the time to ask him, when Natalie's letter had jolted them from their well-defended positions.

Perdita asked crisply, 'Why did you marry me, Luke?'

'It seemed the best way out of an intolerable situation.'

'Of course.' Well, nothing ventured, nothing gained didn't actually promise any sort of victory. The element of risk that marked all her dealings with Luke meant that she would always be in danger of being hurt.

'And that's a lie,' he said savagely, turning around to look at her. 'I married you because I wanted you. I've always wanted you. You walked in through the door after ten years away and it was all there again, the hunger in my gut, the bloody itch in my groin——'

'Stop it!' She whirled, clapping her hands over her ears, but he caught them and dragged them down, forcing her around to face him.

'You wanted to know,' he said angrily. 'At first I hated it and hated you, because you're the only woman in the world with that power. What happened all those years ago was a nightmare, it destroyed my self-esteem, but as soon as you came back I could see it happening again. You wouldn't go, you wouldn't be warned off or threatened away, and I felt that same sick helpless craving crawl through me. So I thought, well, why not? If we were married you'd no longer have this power over me. But first I'd make sure you wouldn't leave the girls. I watched you with them, and it was obvious that they liked you and you were prepared to be sensible with them. So I persuaded you to marry me and looked forward to dulling the edge of this bloody torment.'

'And now that you've done it?' Her voice was cool and remote because she didn't dare let loose the floodgates of emotion that threatened to drown her.

He said with leashed irony, 'Marrying you was the most stupid thing I could have done. I miscalculated completely.'

Perdita stepped back, trying with that small movement to put some symbolic distance between them. Tension sawed through the space between them, shortening her breath, quickening her heartbeat, sending panicky impulses through her. She couldn't speak, couldn't think.

Eyes fixed on her face, he continued roughly, 'It didn't go away. It got worse. At first I told myself it was just sex, that you knew all the tricks, but within a very short

time I realised something I'd been hiding from myself
for the past ten years.'

Although she couldn't bear this, intuition told her that
it was cathartic for him. He was standing by the dressing-
table, looking down at the last of the roses, a pale pink
miniature that Rosie had rescued from the prunings and
nestled into a drift of pink and chalky white, heavily
scented jasmine. His arrogant profile, etched in bronze
against the pale blue walls, wrenched something in her
heart.

'And what,' she asked in the colourless tone of desperation, 'was that?'

He looked at her with eyes where devils were caged.
'I realised that I loved you,' he said calmly, a sardonic
smile thinning his lips. 'Amusing, isn't it? You can laugh
if you want to.'

Sheer frustrated rage boiled up in her. Taking the three
steps that separated them, she swung her arm and caught
him a crack across the cheek, the mark of her hand
standing out like a brand. 'You idiot,' she hissed, steeling
herself against the faint, arousing scent of male. 'If you
love me, why the *hell* didn't you tell me?'

The intent blue of his eyes pierced through the layers
of her composure, the sleek, all-enveloping armour,
seamless and unbreakable, that she had donned to protect
herself from him. As always, that gaze stirred something
in the pit of her stomach, sent a shiver of sensation up
her spine, melted the source of heat between her legs.

'Why?' he asked slowly. 'So that you could laugh?'

'Why would I want to laugh? What normal woman
laughs when the man she has loved for the last twelve
years tells her he loves her? Why do you think I married
you, you overgrown oaf?'

She was crying, the words bursting out between sobs,
tears glazing her eyes.

'Perdita,' he said, and there was a note she had never
heard before in his voice. 'Darling—don't, please don't.
I can't bear it when you cry...'

His arms around her were warm and strong and tender, and she leaned her face into his chest and wept as though her heart would break.

'Darling,' he said thickly, 'my dearest, I didn't know you loved me—how could I? I thought you only married me because you wanted the children.'

'I could have applied for access,' she wept. 'You must have known—I go up in flames when you come near me.'

'How could I know?' he said simply. 'You're a very sensuous woman. Perhaps——'

'Don't you dare say it!'

His strong arms tightened around her; as she wiped her eyes and blew her nose he carried her across to the bed and sat down on the edge, holding her across his lap as though he was never going to let her go.

'Just for your information,' she said, transfixing him with a ferocious green stare, 'I have slept with one other man, and although I liked him very much, it was nothing like—what happens when——'

His eyes were narrowed and fierce. 'You don't have to consider my feelings,' he said, the raw undertone to his voice very apparent. 'I don't like the thought of you making love to anyone else, but I can deal with it.'

'One other man,' she said, barely moving her lips.

'Then what——?' He stopped, and the beautiful, severe mouth relaxed. 'I told myself that I could cope with your other lovers. I lied without even realising it. Some day you must tell me why you got your name linked to so many men, but at the moment I'm rather desperately trying to convince myself that this relief is not the chauvinist possessiveness of a man who wants to own his woman body and soul.'

She smiled adoringly, and a touch smugly, up at him.

'Yes, you may well laugh.' Not even when they had made love had his voice sounded like this, all aloofness fled, the note of reserve banished by a warm sensuality. Arms tightly around her, his head bent so that his breath feathered across her cheek, he said, 'I can't help being possessive, but I'll fight it, I swear.'

'I don't mind if you're a little bit demanding.'

'All right, a little bit.'

Natalie had tried to reach beyond the grave and divide them. Perdita almost hated her for doing it, and yet she understood her cousin much better now, the demons that had driven her so that in the end she had almost destroyed everyone she loved.

'I can't believe that you love me,' she murmured.

'Is it so difficult?' He held her a little away, capturing her gaze, his own deep and intense and compelling. 'You've brought me peace, and laughter, a serenity I've never experienced, and a divine restlessness. Can you believe that, Perdita?'

She looked up into eyes that were no longer the icy hue of shattered glass. He was gazing at her with naked pleading, as though he didn't dare press her any further.

'Oh, Luke,' she said, smiling, 'I have to, because I think it would kill me if you lied.'

'I swear, I'll never lie to you again,' he promised in the deep, tender voice of a lover, and began to kiss her.

Later that night, when the twins were in bed and the fire burnt high in the grate, Perdita's eyes fell on the portrait of Natalie's smiling face. Unconsciously, she snuggled deeper into Luke's arms.'

'You can get rid of it if you want to,' he said.

'No. She's no threat to me now. I was just thinking, I didn't know her at all, really.'

'None of us knew Natalie. She had to work hard to be so charming. She trained herself to be the perfect wife for the perfect man. Most of the time she coped well with the impossible standards she set herself, but every so often the mask would slip and the gears would show.'

Thoughtfully, Perdita said, 'She must have hated herself.'

'Yes,' he said slowly, a note of surprise in his voice. 'I think she did, and her hatred was compounded when she realised she couldn't have children. There was no medical reason for her inability to conceive. I tried to convince her that it needn't make any difference, that I loved her, but my love wasn't enough. In time, I came to see that she hadn't so much married me as a man who could fit in with that perfect life she'd visualised.'

'Poor Natalie.' Perdita kissed his throat.

'Yes. When you became pregnant she must have felt that her plans had been vindicated by success.' A lingering undertone of shock in his words convinced her, although she no longer needed it, that he had been telling her the truth.

Perdita asked inconsequentially, 'What did she tell you when she got back from the Gardiners' the next day?'

'She simply said that the hotel couldn't have given her message to me, and when I told her you'd gone back to your mother she said that it was a pity, but perhaps it was for the best.'

Perdita buried her face in the warm column of his throat, inhaling deeply, taking his special scent into her lungs. 'I thought she loved me,' she whispered.

'She did, as far as she was able to love anyone.'

'Did you know—what she was like?'

His arms tightened. His heart beat steadily against her, comforting with its regularity, although, she noticed with a tiny edge of anticipation, its speed was picking up. 'No,' he said. 'I didn't understand how close she'd come to the edge of madness. When the children came she stepped back from that brink. She must have convinced herself that they really were hers, and so she was able to forget what she'd done.'

'She could have harmed them.' It was a thought that had been prowling around the borders of her mind all afternoon, a fear she hadn't been able to articulate.

'No. Being the perfect woman means that you have to be the perfect mother,' Luke said.

But Perdita couldn't accept that. Unable to drag her mind away from the streak of madness showing through the façade of Natalie's sanity, she wondered whether the children had been abused in subtle, secret ways that would only reveal themselves later in life.

'Stop it!' he commanded, apparently understanding the way her mind was heading. 'Yes, it occurred to me too, but you know them; do they seem to you to have been damaged?'

'No,' she said thickly, clutching at her composure. 'No, of course they don't.'

'She wanted them to be happy, to be a credit to her,' he said. 'She read all the books, did all the right things. They were good children, which made it easier.'

Repressing with a shiver the question of what might have happened to the children had they not been good, Perdita allowed her jealousy to drive her into an unwise comment. 'You loved her very much.'

'Yes, I loved her.' His voice was steady. 'Not in the same way as I love you. I was twenty-one when we were married, she was a couple of years older, and I felt a young man's dazzled love for her. I'm no longer young, or untried, or callow. I love you with everything that I am, everything I can possibly be. I can't prove to you that I love you more, my heart's dearest, except by living with you and showing you exactly what you mean to me every day, until in the end you accept it.'

She pulled away, looking into his face. Unerringly, he had hit on the one thing that still nagged at her. He wasn't smiling, but the hard, distant self-sufficiency had gone, replaced by a warmth that spoke more to her than his words could.

She realised how petty she was being, how she was letting the rejection of her childhood affect her. Smiling, she surrendered the last of her defences, and leaned forward to kiss his chin. 'I do accept it,' she said quietly. 'I know you love me. I love you, too, and we'll make a happy life together.'

His mouth came down on hers, hard and fierce and possessive, a vow and a claim together. When he lifted his head the eagle's light was back in his eyes. 'Let's go up to bed,' he said.

EPILOGUE

'ALL right, try to look responsible,' the photographer commanded. 'You're not going to drop those babies, so stop looking so terrified!'

Olivia and Rosalind clutched their burdens even more closely. The oddly assorted adults around smiled. Toni Hansen, who used to be Perdita's agent in New York, said to her husband, 'Think I should sign up the taller one—Olivia, isn't it—right now? She's just gorgeous, isn't she?'

He was eyeing his champagne with respect. Vintage, and one of the best houses. He hadn't expected to come across that sort of thing at the furthest ends of the earth. 'Not a hope,' he said shrewdly. 'If she's interested you'll probably have to wait until she's twenty. That's one protective family.'

'Pity.' She continued to survey the group as they shuffled into place. Clearly Perdita had fallen on her feet. Four years had put on a little weight, which suited her, and the look she gave that overwhelming husband of hers scorched through decorum. Toni allowed herself her sole sentimental sigh for the year.

On her books were some of the most beautiful men in the world. No one could call Luke Dennison beautiful, but whenever he walked into a room everyone knew it. He had presence, that rare amalgam of confidence and masculinity and authority that so few men could boast. He'd photograph well too, she thought, scrutinising him professionally. Great bones.

And there was no doubt that he was head over heels in love with his wife. Not that he wore his emotions on his face, but a couple of times she'd intercepted a glance,

183

and the elemental intensity of his strange eyes as they rested on his wife made her stomach curl.

The possessive sort, she decided, but if Perdita didn't mind, who cared? Besides, he apparently had no chauvinist objections to Perdita working; last night he'd boasted a little about how well the landscaping business was going. If the garden here was any indication, Perdita had great talent. The place looked glorious.

Shuddering at the thought of those exquisite hands in the dirt, Toni looked critically on as the photographer took photo after photo of the two sons of the family in their sisters' arms.

Not that Perdita would be dirtying her hands for a good few months to come. A nurse was all very well, but twins were going to keep her busy.

'Have you noticed,' she said out of the corner of her mouth, 'that the boys have the same coloured hair as their sisters?'

'So?'

'It just struck me as funny.' But if that taller daughter wasn't Perdita's she would eat her deliciously frivolous hat.

'Lots of things strike you as funny,' he said cheerfully.

She shrugged. Whatever had happened in the past, they were certainly one big, happy family now. The girls idolised Perdita—as well they should, she was a darling to them—and clearly adored their new brothers.

'Are you planning to have any more children?' she asked an hour later, when Perdita had come back after feeding the babies.

'Well, no. The doctors couldn't swear that I wouldn't have another set of twins, so we decided that four was enough.'

Toni grinned her famous shark's smile. 'Yeah, babe,' she said in a gravelly voice. 'Better not push your luck. Well, here's congratulations. I thought you were crazy giving up everything, but it looks as though it's worked out for you.'

Perdita's gaze caught Luke's. He lifted his glass to her, and came across. Her heart flipped; she loved him so much. Each year that passed brought an increase in trust and happiness.

Later that night, when the girls were in bed, she went up to kiss them goodnight. They had been marvellous, both as hostesses and nursemaids.

Following the sound of voices, she walked into Olivia's room. Both looked up sharply as she came in, and Rosie said from her perch on the end of the bed, 'Go on, Liv, you ask her.'

'Ask me what?'

Strangely enough each girl wore an identical expression, one in which excitement and unease were equally mixed. For a moment neither spoke, then Rosie blurted, 'We wondered whether you were our real mother, our birth mother.'

The words fell into a pit of silence. As Rosie clapped her hand over her mouth, eyes the exact colour of her mother's widened above her palm.

'Yes, I am.' Perdita sounded calm, belying the intense pounding of her heart.

'And Daddy is our real father?'

Perdita nodded.

'Then that means——' Olivia stopped.

Perdita sat down and explained what had happened, leaving out everything but bare circumstances of the mistaken identity. Both girls flushed with embarrassment, yet their fascination was evident.

'It sounds like a fairy-story,' Rosie exclaimed.

With a few too many coincidences. Perdita smiled. 'Yes,' she said, 'and like a fairy-story everyone but you had a guilty secret, and suffered a lot of pain.'

Both girls nodded. 'Do you mind that we don't call you Mum?' Olivia asked suddenly.

Perdita shook her head. 'No. You know who brought you up, and naturally you call her Mother.' She hesitated, then asked, 'What made you suspect that I might be your birth mother?'

The sisters exchanged complicated looks before Olivia said, 'When you had the twins. They've got our red hair, and although I look a bit like Mum's photograph, I look a lot more like you. And Rosie's got your eyes. It all seemed to add up. Then today Mrs Hansen said I had your bones.'

Rosie flushed deeply. 'Ages ago I came into your bedroom when you were showering, and you'd left your locket on the dressing table and I peeped in, and saw the locks of hair there. I felt awful about it, so I didn't tell you, but when the boys were born I remembered.'

'Ah, I see.' Perdita took the locket from around her neck and flicked it open, holding it out so that both girls could see the two fine, soft locks of red hair, the identical shade to their brothers'.

'Is it ours?' Olivia breathed.

Perdita nodded. 'Yes. I cut it off from the back of your heads the day I left the home.'

'Why didn't you tell Dad you were having us?'

Tricky ground here. Perdita said, 'How could I? He loved your mother, and she loved him. What had happened was a horrendous mistake. I didn't want to break your mother's heart, although if I'd known that she couldn't have children I might have told them. And I couldn't keep you. I was too young and too silly and too poor. So I cut off the locks of your hair and cried myself into exhaustion.'

She didn't know that her expression mirrored some of the desolation of that time until Rosie leapt to her feet and flung her arms around her, hugging her tightly. 'Never mind,' she soothed. 'Don't cry, Perdita, it was all for the best, really, wasn't it?'

Olivia had scrambled from beneath her sheets; she pressed her cheek against Perdita's, adding her unspoken comfort.

Perdita sniffed, and groped for a handkerchief. For once she had one. She had anguished so much over these revelations that now it all seemed far too easy. 'It wasn't your father's fault, or mine. It was a terrible mistake, yet out of it came great happiness.'

Rosie smiled at her. 'Well, it's different from a fairy-tale, because there's no wicked stepmother.'

Perdita's gaze moved to Olivia's face. 'It's all nicely tied up,' her oldest daughter by half an hour said, smiling. 'I'm glad you and Dad are our real parents. It means we won't have to look for you.'

Back in her own bedroom, Perdita told Luke what had happened. 'They decided not to tell anyone,' she said, yawning as he slid the zip fastener down her back. 'They felt there'd be too many questions asked, and that it would be more fun to have it our secret. I hope our boys grow up to be as wonderful as their sisters.'

'I'm sure they will.' He kissed the back of her neck. 'Your father and stepmother seemed to enjoy them-selves.'

'Yes, I think they did.'

After they'd been married a year Luke had suggested she approach her father. Perdita had resisted, but eventually the need to know had won, and he had ar-ranged a meeting. To her shocked surprise, Francis Meredith had been the unknown man at her mother's funeral.

'I should have looked for you,' he said. 'I didn't. I'd have had to go behind my wife's back, and I wasn't going to hurt her any more than I already had. I took the easy way out, and I don't blame you for despising me.'

But Perdita couldn't despise this man who had been so patently glad to see her. She shook her head.

'But believe me,' he continued, 'I tried to persuade your mother to accept an allowance, a house to live in. She refused everything, and in the end I got tired of offering, and she moved again, and I lost touch. Then

I saw her name in the newspaper, and went to the funeral. I thought you'd be still at school, and I hoped
that I'd be able to look after you. But you were sleek
and sophisticated and obviously doing well, and I realised
it was too late. I didn't know what your mother had told
you—but I must admit that concern for my wife was the
main reason I didn't make greater efforts to keep in
contact. She was ill, and she hated your mother.'

For good reason, Perdita had to admit.

'If I'd brought home a stepdaughter I doubt whether
she'd have been able to cope. I still feel wretched about
everything,' her father said. 'I behaved very badly. But
sometimes we're given a second chance.'

They would never be close friends, but the relationship was warm and pleasant; even his wife had accepted her, now that she was no threat. And it probably
helped, Perdita thought cynically, that she had married
Luke!

She shivered as her husband's teeth closed gently on
a certain sensitive spot at the juncture of her neck and
shoulder.

'Mm, I do love you,' she murmured, turning into his
arms, her green eyes slumbrous.

'You must be tired.' He lifted her and put her on the
bed.

She gave a smoky little laugh, pulling him down beside
her. 'How can I be? None of you will let me do any
work. Rosie allowed me to hold each of the boys while
she and Olivia dealt with the other, and that's the sum
total of work I've done today. I promise, I'm not in the
least tired.'

'Good.' His pale eyes heated, tenderness mingling with
the glitter of desire she had come to know so well. 'I
love you,' he said, kissing along the line of her jaw from
her ear to her chin.

In her last coherent thought before the honeyed fire
swept her away, Perdita decided that the greatest gamble

of her life had been more than worth the element of risk. Natalie's ghost had been robbed of its power to hurt or to harm. Here, in Luke's arms, in his heart, she was safe, as he was in hers.

BRIDE'S
BAY RESORT

UNLOCK THE DOOR TO GREAT ROMANCE
AT BRIDE'S BAY RESORT

Join Harlequin's new across-the-lines series, set in an exclusive hotel on an island off the coast of South Carolina.

Seven of your favorite authors will bring you exciting stories about fascinating heroes and heroines discovering love at Bride's Bay Resort.

Look for these fabulous stories coming to a store near you beginning in January 1996.

Harlequin American Romance #613 in January
Matchmaking Baby by Cathy Gillen Thacker

Harlequin Presents #1794 in February
Indiscretions by Robyn Donald

Harlequin Intrigue #362 in March
Love and Lies by Dawn Stewardson

Harlequin Romance #3404 in April
Make Believe Engagement by Day Leclaire

Harlequin Temptation #588 in May
Stranger in the Night by Roseanne Williams

Harlequin Superromance #695 in June
Married to a Stranger by Connie Bennett

Harlequin Historicals #324 in July
Dulcie's Gift by Ruth Langan

Visit Bride's Bay Resort each month wherever Harlequin books are sold.

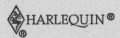

HARLEQUIN®

BBAYG

MILLION DOLLAR SWEEPSTAKES

You're About to Become a *Privileged Woman*

Reap the rewards of fabulous free gifts and benefits with proofs-of-purchase from Harlequin and Silhouette books

Pages & Privileges™

It's our way of thanking you for buying our books at your favorite retail stores.

Pages & Privileges ™

✂

PROOF OF PURCHASE

HP-PP120

Offer expires October 31, 1996

Harlequin and Silhouette— the most privileged readers in the world!

For more information about Harlequin and Silhouette's PAGES & PRIVILEGES program call the Pages & Privileges Benefits Desk: 1-503-794-2499

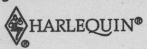

HARLEQUIN®

HP-PP120